It's almost time. He takes a deep breath to stop the tickling in his eyes, like he is going to cry. Babies cry, his mother . . . she used to cry. When he thinks of her, he feels even more like crying, but that's weakness, and he is committed to power. Only for a second does he remember that he's just a kid. He doesn't have to do this.

A kid, yes, but he has the power within him to kill the joy inside the hulking old building. The couple from the car go to join the others. It's time. He knows it without knowing why. He moves out of the shadows and walks toward the steep flight of stairs into the building. He feels no chill now, no more anger, no fear. He is powerful. . . .

Please turn to the back of the book for an interview with Joyce Christmas.

By Joyce Christmas
Published by Fawcett Books:

MOOD TO MURDER

A Betty Trenka Mystery

Joyce Christmas

FAWCETT GOLD MEDAL • NEW YORK

A Fawcett Gold Medal Book
Published by The Ballantine Publishing Group
Copyright © 1999 by Joyce Christmas

www.randomhouse.com/BB/

Library of Congress Catalog Card Number: 99-90218

ISBN 0-449-15012-7

Manufactured in the United States of America

First Ballantine Books Edition: June 1999

10 9 8 7 6 5 4 3 2 1

Once again, for my
Constant Reader,
Larry Chervenak

PROLOGUE

IT IS quiet here in the shadows with the slow breath of spring air fluttering a lock of hair, kissing a youthful cheek feverish with anticipation. A scrap of paper dances slowly across the gritty parking lot. There are stars up there in the heavens, there is music for slow dancing beyond this dark corner. Light shines on the sandy playground through tall, grime-clouded windows, making a splash of brightness that doesn't reach the black trees along its boundary.

Goosebumps rise on a youthful arm, but the chill comes from within, not from the night. It's warm out, as warm as the first day of May should be. The chill comes from fear of what has already happened and what will soon be done, or maybe just knowing that it must be done at all. And it's the right thing to do, the only thing to do to calm the river of hatred that is raging through his blood. Blood is everywhere, and soon there will be more.

They're all inside now, swooning in each other's arms on the dance floor, now thrashing through an orgy of throbbing heavy metal and rock on a festival for May Day. What had Raven called it? Beltane, a witches' feast day, a day of power for those who can seize it for themselves. She talks girl talk about magic and spells but that means

1

nothing. It's power and control that works in the real
world, that's what Brad says, and he is always right. The
boy tells himself to be calm and sure and in control. Any
sign of weakness will make him lose the power he is about
to grasp. Forget everything except this moment.

He closes his eyes for a minute and listens to the music.
It is loud and clear in the night. In the darkness behind his
eyelids, he can see the enemy exploding in jagged flashes
of color. Pow, pow. It is as vivid as a video game, the kind
where if you keep scoring more hits, you quickly move to
higher and higher levels. This is the game that will make
him a champion.

A car drives into the parking lot. Latecomers. The girl
wears a yellow dress. He freezes as she gets out. Yellow
dress and red hair. He doesn't even dare to breathe. He
knows her, even if she refuses to know him. He recognizes
her date too, the big kid who's a junior, and who hangs out
with Brad at the pizza shop, where they talk in low voices
the others can't hear and laugh at private jokes.

It's almost time. He takes a deep breath to stop the tickling
in his eyes, like he is going to cry. Babies cry, his mother . . .
she used to cry. When he thinks of her, he feels even more
like crying, but that's weakness, and he is committed to
power. Only for a second does he remember that he's just a
kid. He doesn't have to do this.

A kid, yes, but he has the power within him to kill the
joy inside the hulking old building. The couple from the
car go to join the others. It's time. He knows it without
knowing why. He moves out of the shadows and walks
toward the steep flight of stairs into the building. He feels
no chill now, no more anger, no fear. He is powerful.

A slight figure, he is wearing a neat dark blazer and gray

trousers, all dressed up like the rest of them, ready to become one of them if someone turns him away from his chosen task. Just for a moment, he betrays his determination by wishing that someone will turn him away. But no one knows what's in his mind, no one understands.

Somewhere beyond the top of the stairs lies release from his unhappiness, his anger, his grief. He isn't afraid now; he's on his way, and someone will pay for his anguish.

A second car pulls into the parking lot, and its lights catch him as he stands at the foot of the stairs. As it pulls into a parking space, he bounds up the steps and enters through the heavy door.

He stands at the end of the long familiar corridor and listens to the music coming from the gymnasium at the end of the hallway. Somebody has draped the doorway with multicolored ribbons and bunches of spring flowers. Decorations for May Day. Mayday. That's a distress call. His father told him that. It's used in the military when the guys need help.

Mayday. Help me. I am dying, we are all dying.

No one can help me now. No one wants to help.

He walks slowly toward the big room full of dancing couples.

Mayday.

Then a voice says, "I can help you if you'll let me. I'm a little late, but I know all about it. Let me help." It is an old, wise, familiar voice. He turns to it eagerly. Mayday.

CHAPTER 1

BETTY TRENKA entered the month of April with joy in her heart, an unexpected surge of optimism, and no sense that the center would not hold. The feeling stayed with her until late in the month, when she woke one Tuesday morning with a special sense of elation. A warm breeze fluttered the bedroom curtains; she could hear birds singing out in the blue spruces and the sturdy old red maple. Behind the slats of the half-lowered venetian blind lurked the bright morning sun. A perfect day, a day full of charm.

All was well in her adopted town of East Moulton, Connecticut. She looked out the window to discover a world of golden light and blue skies. The crocuses along the cement walk from Timberhill Road to her cozy little house had pushed their heads through the earth. Where had they come from, these cheerful buds? She certainly hadn't planted them to decorate her first spring away from her old home near Hartford, her first sad spring away from her comfortable job at Edwards & Son, snatched from her by a forced retirement. She wouldn't think about that now; it only made her mad to consider the power that one selfish and unthinking man had over her life. Sid Edwards Junior wasn't half the man his father was, yet he had made a mockery of the long years both she and Sid Senior had put into the company. Out the door. Now. And that was the end of more than three decades on the job.

She turned her attention back to the crocuses. The bulbs must be the work of the previous owner, who had been far more domesticated than she. Pale green leaves had feathered the trees that masked Ted Kelso's stone house across the road. Ted was working on his garden today. He'd told her that someone was coming in to help him check on how his three hives of bees had survived the winter.

The shouts of the three Saks boys next door and across the field that separated her house from theirs suggested that they, too, felt released from winter's captivity.

It was a day to get something done.

"Something good is going to happen," Betty said seriously to Tina, but the cat merely (and typically) yawned in boredom, stretched languidly, and hopped off the bed to make her way downstairs to the food bowl. Tina made a point of ignoring Betty, with whom she did not much get along, unless it was a question of meals.

"I didn't ask to own you," Betty said, "but I did take you in." Tina was off about the morning's business. Even if she wasn't coddled as she had been in her former life, it was, Betty thought, a pretty good life for a cat. It wasn't all that bad for Betty either. She had enough money, she had a roof over her head, the day was fine. She was determined to see the good side of things.

Betty showered and dressed quickly, then followed Tina downstairs.

With the cat fed and a cup of good coffee before her, Betty sat at the little kitchen table and tried to plan her day. She had no freelance typing jobs, no résumés to reprioritize, no tapes to transcribe, no manuscripts to type, nothing. This was a day when Betty actually felt distressed that she wasn't the sort to pick up a shovel, turn over the earth, and plant some seeds, or paint a fence, or rake up twigs and dead grass. Useful, homeowner-type things.

"We'll just see about that," she said aloud. She was not going to let this day sift away through her fingers like sand. If she no longer had an office to go to, with papers to shuffle and important letters to write, she wasn't going to let her buoyant feelings die on the vine. She'd get advice from Ted on what to plant in the narrow strip of garden left to her by the previous owner of the house.

She'd even been surreptitiously watching a few gardening programs on television, and had found Martha Stewart's enthusiasm for plants and trellises and compost oddly inspiring, although she always turned the set off when Martha started in on Things to Do with Ribbon. She'd almost convinced herself to buy some paint and brighten up the makeshift fence that had been erected to blot out the fire-ruined remains of the old garage she had no intention of replacing.

The smell of spring continued to waft through the house from the open door and windows of the kitchen, and in spite of her sixty-plus years, she could feel the season bubbling in her blood.

Her friend Miho, the Japanese orchid grower who lived out on the road to the mall, had said she sold flats of garden plants every spring at her roadside stand, even before the vegetables from her big garden were ready. That was an answer that appealed to Betty. She wouldn't have to wait for seeds to sprout and plants to grow and flower. Besides, she enjoyed visiting with the quiet young woman, who wasn't especially popular in conservative East Moulton, which didn't much hold with "foreigners."

That category even included Judit, the strange old woman who'd invaded Betty's home a few weeks back, perhaps bent on robbing her, although it hadn't turned out that way. Then Judit decided she and Betty were best friends.

Judit was some sort of refugee from Eastern Europe, but in a sense once-removed. So was Betty, if it came to that. Her Czech ancestors had bravely ventured to the New World of upstate Connecticut a generation or two ago. Betty had persuaded Miho to allow Judit (*you-deet* in her accented pronunciation) to park herself and her battered RV on the edge of Miho's property in exchange for helping out with the vegetables. Judit was at least as out of place in East Moulton as Miho, and while she wasn't truly Betty's Best Friend, Betty got a kind of kick out of hearing Judit describe her travels about the world and rather less of a kick from hearing about the burdens of caring for her rough and rather frightening grandsons. Thankfully "the boys" had taken to the road in their old green pickup, abandoning Judit in East Moulton after terrorizing both her and Betty, who now felt responsible. But for her, Judit would have their companionship still, keeping busy with the cooking and washing that had always been her role in life. Like Betty, Judit had been forcibly retired.

She'd been worried about Judit because she had not looked well when she had last seen her. Well, Judit was an old one, probably a lot older than Betty's sixty-some years, and she'd had a hard, unsettled life. Betty resolved to visit with her today when she drove to Miho's place.

"Instant gratification is what I need," Betty said aloud,

thinking about the boxes of already blooming flowers she'd buy. Tina, who had been curled up in plump splendor in a patch of sun on the kitchen floor, suddenly had enough of her conversation, although it was usually Betty who got impatient with herself for talking to the cat as though she was human. Tina got to her feet, looked at Betty peevishly, then stalked toward the door and looked back over her shoulder, demanding to be allowed out into the spring sunshine.

"Get along, you tiresome beast," Betty said and opened the door. "And don't snack on any birds."

Tina hesitated, then scampered down the steps into the tall, scraggly grass of the backyard. Betty sighed. She'd have to find someone to mow the grass in front and back regularly over the next few months. It was too much for her to do. Maybe the young man who helped Ted would be willing to help out.

Ted had described Brad Melville as a good worker if a bit "different." When Betty had asked for a definition of "different," Ted said that Brad hated being stuck in a small town like East Moulton, where people didn't understand him.

"What's to understand?"

Ted had shrugged and said, "He looks different. He doesn't really work except for odd jobs. That doesn't sit well with our industrious citizens. He hangs out at the diner or that roadhouse near the highway with bikers and truckers. He doesn't have much money, although he always has a scheme to accumulate some. He spent quite a bit of time bumming around the country and the world before stopping here. He lived in East Moulton for a time as a boy, and rumor has it, used to be in constant trouble. I don't believe he still has any connections left in town, but he came back this past winter, says it's the closest to a home he knows. The town, of course, has a long collective memory. People don't want to admit he's a grown man now; to them he's still the bad boy of fifteen years ago. He's quite intelligent. At least he seems to grasp what my bees need, he knows how to dig a hole, and he reads."

"All the important stuff," Betty remarked. "Bees and books."

Ted had also mentioned that Brad was a minor celebrity in town, because he quickly became a hero to the local boys, who eagerly listened to his tales of life on the road in dangerous and exotic places. He was (naturally) considered a bad influence by East Moulton's adults because of his past history. Even so, the kids often helped him with his various odd jobs.

That's settled, Betty thought. One of Brad's boys could certainly push a lawn mower for her if Brad wouldn't.

She put on a light denim jacket in case it wasn't as warm as it seemed, although except for that one snowstorm, it had been a mostly mild winter. She headed across Timberhill Road to Ted's place to ask him for suggestions on what she should plant that would please his bees, while at the same time not being too much trouble for her to care for.

An unfamiliar car parked in Ted's driveway suggested that Brad had arrived to do his chores.

Ted disliked having to ask others to assist him, but his wheelchair prevented him from doing the heavy lifting of honey and bee-filled combs that hive maintenance required.

"I don't get much honey," he'd told her, "and I don't

really have the equipment to extract it anyhow, but ob-
serving bee life entertains me."

She remembered that he'd urged her to plant things that
would offer his bees nectar and pollen beyond his own
yard. "Your pine trees give them honeydew, that's something, but they're willing to roam widely to find flowers."
And then he'd explained in rather too much detail about
the habits of honeybees and their life cycle, the mating of
the queen, the busy workers, the tasks of the drones, the
care of the growing brood, the rest. One good thing about
Ted was that once he explained something in depth, he
didn't do it a second time. He expected you to remember.
The bee lecture was a thing of the past.

Timberhill Road was empty of traffic as usual, since it
didn't lead much of anywhere, except to Crispin Abbott's
spacious and recently renovated house and old Alida's
even more spacious home.

After Alida's lovely landscaped grounds, the land became heavily wooded and the road meandered through the
trees until it reached the county road that led back to East
Moulton center. She hoped Tina had sense enough to stay
in the yard and out of the street.

She peered into the dusty car in Ted's driveway—the
backseat was crammed with cardboard cartons, out of
which spilled dingy T-shirts, an old sneaker, and yes, even
a few books. She rounded the corner of the stone house
and entered the garden area.

Masses of crocuses were already in bloom here, making
vivid patches of bright yellow and purple. There were
nodding white snowdrops, and some clusters of daffodils
and tulips, with buds ready to burst into bloom. In a shady
corner near the house, purple and white violets and a fra-

grant bed of lily-of-the-valley had already come to life, and she could hear the faint buzz of bees hard at work checking out the garden.

Ted was sitting in his wheelchair at the far end of the garden, near the row of white hives. He was pointing out something to a tall person decked out in white coveralls with elastic around the wrists and ankles. She couldn't see his face because he wore a hat with netting, just as in pictures she'd seen of beekeepers. She supposed that bees were likely to be cranky if disturbed from their end-of-winter doze.

"Good morning," she called. "I hope I'm not going to be in the way. I had a couple of silly questions."

"Elizabeth, come right on over. No question of yours is too silly. Just a minute while Brad checks on the queen in the first hive. A little smoke to keep them calm, Brad." Brad squeezed out some puffs of white smoke from a device he carried, and leaned toward the hive. "That's right. The brood is in the bottom flat, remember, the queen above." Brad directed a few more puffs of smoke at the open back of the hive and extracted a flat of honeycomb. Ted wheeled himself along the smooth flagstone path to examine it. "Have a look at this, Betty. I hope you're not allergic to bee stings."

"I'm not," Betty said, "as far as I know." She peered at the comb where the cells appeared to be sealed with wax. Clusters of lethargic bees clung to the comb, but a few flew about the hive buzzing in annoyance.

"The queen's been laying already. Brood looks promising, and we haven't been invaded by mice or wasps over the winter," Ted said. "This is Brad Melville, Elizabeth. I think I've mentioned what a help he is to me. Elizabeth

Trenka, Brad. Okay, you can put the flat back. Get rid of the debris at the entrance, will you? And we can go on to the next hive."

Brad replaced the flat and took off his veiled hat. He was dark-haired, with a lean, brooding face that might be called striking, but his eyes were distinctly alarming. They had very black irises in startling contrast to the whites of his eyes. Betty thought they looked like the glass eyes one saw in the masks of Egyptian mummies. He could be younger than he looked, but she thought he was probably in his twenties. That would be logical for someone who had traveled around the world. Now she noticed his thin, cruel-looking mouth.

"How do you do, ma'am?" At least he was polite, even as he looked her over with something like insolence.

Betty tried to remember if she'd ever seen him around East Moulton. He was certainly too old to be one of the teenaged boys who attended the reading group on the day she volunteered at the town library, but she would be the first to admit that most young people looked about the same to her. Nikes, jeans and T-shirts, whatever their age. But she would have remembered Brad and those eyes if she'd ever come face-to-face with him.

"Do you have time to get out the tiller and turn over the dirt in that bed in the corner?" Ted asked. "I want to sow some new stuff. Clover maybe. The bees like clover. We can put off looking at the other hives until tomorrow."

"I got plenty of time," Brad said. "Raven was supposed to hitch a ride and meet me here half an hour ago, but she's never been on time in her life. She's always running into some guy she wants to put a spell on." He looked at Betty steadily for a long moment, until she felt quite unnerved. It was his eyes that bothered her. "The old one is feeling pain," he said, so softly that she strained to hear him. "She has been toying with matters which are not her business. The cards . . ."

"What do you mean?" Betty said nervously, but Brad turned on his heel, and went off to the storage shed, soon to reappear with a wheeled tiller. He proceeded to tear up the dirt at the end of the garden without another word.

"What was that all about?" Ted asked. "Are you all right? You look . . . bedazzled."

"Yes—no. I mean, what an odd thing for him to say. I was just thinking about Judit, and there he was talking about her, saying she was in pain."

Ted laughed. "Your old lady friend who tried to rob you? How do you figure that's who he was talking about?"

"She didn't try to rob me," Betty said indignantly. "She was in trouble because of her grandsons, and I helped her. He said 'the old one' and mentioned pain and the cards. I told you Judit fancies herself a card reader. I know she hasn't been feeling well, and when he said 'pain' . . . Well, I have been thinking about her, and he knew it."

"So you imagine that he read your mind? I admit he's an unusual young man. The kids are devoted to him, because he takes them camping and stuff, and fills their heads with wild stories, but I don't think his skills run to mind reading. I daresay Raven wouldn't put up with that. She wouldn't like him looking into her mind."

"Raven?" She looked at Ted. "I've heard that name."

"She's his girlfriend, lives in town—actually with Brad, much to the dismay of our upright and moral citizens. A rather scary young woman, if you ask me, but most women scare me," Ted said, "except you. You are merely terrifying in your wisdom and efficiency."

"Oh, Ted . . ." But she was flattered. "I think I do know something of Raven. Molly mentioned her, not with much approval, and pointed her out to me. I think she's even come into the library."

Molly Perkins was ground zero for the town's gossip, standing guard over the pharmacy on Main Street owned by her husband, the pharmacist, and paying attention to every detail of East Moulton's life. "Raven's tall, with long black hair and long red nails." Ted nodded. "A little too much of an exotic for East Moulton. Looks as though she doesn't eat properly, too pale to be entirely healthy, but that may be because of bad makeup advice."

"You've got her down just right," Ted said. "A bright girl, though."

"Ah. Does she also read? Well, she must if I've seen her at the library. Never mind. Maybe you'll give me some advice. I've decided to give up on not caring about domestic matters and pretend that I do. I decided today to plant a little garden out at the back of my house. Now I need to know from you what I should plant."

"Lobelia, salvia, petunias, marigolds, impatiens. Big, fat pansies are nice. Start with the easy stuff. I suggest you see Miho; she's sure to have flats of everything already planted and growing, ready to pop into the ground. Put a couple of geraniums in pots on your back doorstep, hang some baskets of fuchsia. You can plant a forsythia bush and a lilac tree for next season, and put in tulip and daffodil bulbs in the fall. Well, you know about them. Then you can occupy yourself over the summer wielding a hose and pulling weeds. I'll even volunteer Brad to push my chair over to your house so I can continue to give you advice."

Betty suddenly felt guilty that she had put off having a graded ramp installed so Ted could manage his wheelchair up to her house. Something else she'd definitely see to over the next few months. She'd enjoy having Ted visit her instead of always visiting him, although she certainly wouldn't dare to cook a meal for him. But she might offer him a cup of coffee. That was something she'd mastered.

"I'd be grateful for any help I can get," Betty said. "It's not too early to plant things, is it?"

"It's okay, April's almost over," he said. "The warming trend is here to stay. Everything is a bit ahead of itself this year anyhow because the winter was so mild."

"I'll run up to Miho this afternoon. It will give me a chance to see how Judit is doing. She and Miho certainly appear to get along."

"Hmm. A Japanese and a Gypsy. Odd combination for our little town."

"Judit isn't a Gypsy," Betty said. The old woman certainly was odd, however. And judging by her grandsons, who seemed to fit the stereotype for Gypsies and had departed for parts unknown, perhaps they all really were Gypsy wanderers, complete with fortune-telling cards.

"I like her," Betty said. "She's old and vulnerable. She didn't mean me any harm, and she's all alone. Sort of like me."

"Don't go gloomy on me," Ted said. "It's too nice a day. I'm feeling very up today."

"So was I," Betty said, "until your friend Brad gave me a chill with his mind-reading. Still, mornings like this make the world seem right and everything possible. Oh, there's one more thing. I need to line up someone to mow my grass this spring and summer. I thought maybe Brad . . ." She stopped. She found herself not really eager to have that young man about her house, staring at her with those eyes of his and reading her mind.

"I don't know that Brad would condescend to such a basic task. He fancies himself a more elevated practitioner of manual labor, but his followers will do his bidding in an instant. We'll find you someone. Aha! Are you ready for this? Here's Raven."

CHAPTER 2

ALMOST A twin of Brad, Raven was, and as deathly pale as Betty remembered, but that might have been an effect caused by her black hair, black shirt, black jeans, and pouty bright red lips and nails.

"Hiya, Ted. I see you got Brad sweating out the toxins of modern life." She waved at Brad, who barely acknowledged her and kept on turning over the soil.

"Nice day, isn't it, Raven?" Ted said. "I want you to meet my neighbor, Elizabeth Trenka. Elizabeth, this is Brad's friend, Raven."

"My pleasure," Raven said, and fiddled with a silver pendant on a chain around her neck. "Haven't I seen you at the library?"

"Oh, yes, of course. I'm there on Wednesdays." So she did read. Betty remembered her gazing at the shelves, and even checking out a few books. She was fond of science fiction and fantasy and historical romances.

"Is Brad almost ready to leave?" Raven asked. "We got some people who are coming around to see us. Only kids, but we have this discussion group, and . . . well, they stayed out of school today, so we ought to be on time. I have to get stuff ready."

Betty didn't approve of children skipping school. She tried to remember if she'd ever cut school without her parents' permission. Things were different half a century ago. You went to school unless you had chicken pox or measles, and that was that. She'd certainly never missed a day's work without a good excuse, not that Sid Edwards would have begrudged her time off whenever she wanted it, but she wasn't one to get sick more than once a year if that, and if she wasn't contagious, she'd shown up at Edwards & Son no matter how she felt.

Even these days, with a few arthritis pains to slow her down, she'd give anything to be back at the office with a real job to do. She hated being without a definite place in life, and running an office was what she did best.

"Brad's about done for today," Ted said. "Anything more can be finished tomorrow." Neither of them seemed to notice that Betty had retreated into her own thoughts about the good old days when she had a real purpose in life. Now she was thinking about poor Sid, lying in a nursing home all alone. She shouldn't be thinking of gardens and painting fences. She should be on the road to see him. She was sure his children didn't bother to visit him often, but her own weekly visits since February had not been entirely satisfying.

Overall he was making a fair recovery from his stroke, and he always seemed glad to see her, but he was still far from well. The attendants told her that he was stubborn and willful, sometimes refusing to participate in his therapy sessions. But whenever she saw him, he was mostly withdrawn and sad. No stubbornness or willfulness to be seen. Perhaps the routine of the nursing home, along with the stroke and other griefs, had deadened his will to live, along with the affection he had felt and shown toward her when they were working side by side for all those years. Now it was as if she didn't even have that place at his side anymore.

"Don't worry, Miss Trenka, you'll find your place," Raven said, startling Betty. Her voice was low and almost thrilling. "I see that you are on the edge between peace and turmoil. First comes the one and then the other, but I can't say which comes first." Then she strode off to join Brad.

"Ted, I . . ." Suddenly Betty didn't want to have more to do with Brad and Raven, even if it meant failing to recruit one of their minions to mow her lawn. "I have to go now." But she continued to watch the two young people standing side by side at the end of the garden, the girl almost as tall as the man.

Raven and Brad appeared to be communing silently over the patch of churned earth. Then she said something to him that made him draw back in surprise or anger, and he responded by glaring at her and speaking rapidly. Raven stooped quickly and grasped a clump of dirt in her long fingers tipped with violent red. She raised her hand above their heads and allowed the crumbled dirt to fall in a shower on her and Brad.

Brad brushed the dirt from his face, and then he quietly and deliberately slapped her.

Raven took a step back, pointed one lethal finger at him, and looked to be mouthing a string of words that Betty couldn't hear. She imagined that they were not kind words. Ted frowned, then shrugged. "They're always having tiffs," he said. "Raven doesn't do anger management well. And she taunts him often enough, usually about men who find her attractive and would seem to be better prospects than he is."

"Young people today are not what they were in my youth," Betty said. "Of course, my youth occurred in rather more trying times—the Depression and the Second World War, and we were . . . well, different."

Betty remembered that her difference from other girls of her era was that she didn't have a cute, curvy figure that looked good in the dresses of the day, and she was too tall, too awkward, too . . . not pretty to attract boys. Unlike Raven, she never had better prospects—more like no prospects—but that wasn't anything she cared to share with Ted.

"We're going now," Brad said. He wasn't smiling, and his hard, black-and-white eyes wouldn't meet Ted's or Betty's. He seemed to be containing real fury although outwardly he seemed quite calm. Perhaps he was better at anger management than Raven. "I'll be around tomorrow in the afternoon, if that's okay. I think the hives over-wintered okay, and I've seen some bees out checking the lay of the land."

Raven said nothing at all. Betty could see a red mark on her pale cheek where Brad had struck her. She and Ted watched the couple depart.

"I didn't get a chance to ask him about your lawn," Ted said, "but what about the Whiteys? They'd probably rejoice in the chance to earn some money."

The three Saks boys next door to Betty's house, all called Whitey for convenience's sake because of their nearly white blond hair, were under the age of ten, and they didn't strike Betty as serious enough to push a lawn mower, even in shifts, long enough to finish mowing her front and backyards.

"If the Whiteys can't do it, doesn't their mom have a sister in town with a boy about the right age?" Ted asked. "I remember Penny brought him and his mother around here last year for a barbecue I threw for the neighbors. He's fourteen or so, just right for a mower of lawns. Ask Penny."

"That I will," Betty said. "I remember meeting the sister once, Linda, but I don't recall the boy. I suppose it's a good idea to keep the job in the neighborhood, so to speak, and the Whiteys could help him, if he needs help.

"By the way, could I borrow your lawn mower? The old manual one. Mine was incinerated when the garage burned. I meant to buy another and I will, but it wasn't high on my list of priorities until Tina disappeared from view today because the grass is so high."

"Sure," Ted said. "I prefer the way the power mower cuts my grass, so the old clunker doesn't get much work nowadays."

Betty gazed around the pleasant garden, reluctant to leave. Then she said hesitantly, "Ted . . . how . . . how did Raven know I've been worried about finding my place in this new life I've undertaken? And that I was also thinking about how I've lost my place near Sid Senior now that he's so ill and in the nursing home? How did Brad know I was thinking about Judit?"

"They didn't know anything," Ted said sharply. "They just like to play with people. They test out who's gullible and who's not. You're the former, and I am disappointed in you."

His sudden annoyance surprised her, since he was usually even-tempered except when his lack of mobility frustrated him. "I don't want to speculate about Brad and Raven and what they can and can't do," he said. "He's of real use to me, and if I dig too deeply, I stand to lose the best helper I've had in years. Now, you run along and buy your flowers and hire your lawn mower. If Penny's nephew or her kids don't work out, Brad's got a legion to call on, and believe me, when he says 'Jump,' they jump."

CHAPTER 3

BETTY WANDERED back to her house, feeling her enthusiasm for gardening ebbing away. Tina was lurking and pouncing at nothing in the grass on the lawn. It was already looking so overgrown and ragged that she decided she'd better run over to Penny's house and see about the nephew. She could hold off mowing until the weekend certainly, and in the meantime, she herself could manage to pull some of the dandelions that had sprung up overnight.

As she crossed Timberhill Road, in the distance she could see the three Saks boys were gamboling in their yard. Could they too be cutting school? She shook her head, trying to remember what day it was. It wasn't Saturday, she was certain. Saturday was the first of May. Today was Tuesday. Then she wondered if she was getting dangerously forgetful as her years piled up, to the point that she couldn't remember the day of the week. She'd always prided herself on the sharpness of her mind, and hoped that retirement wasn't blunting it.

She walked across the field that separated her house from the Saks place, a sprawling ranch-style house with several recent additions so each boy could have his own room. Penny had already done some spring planting along the side of the house, and Betty was certain there were tomato plants somewhere ready to be put into the ground. The gnarled apple tree in the backyard near the swings and climbing bars was covered with blossoms—Penny liked to boast about her homemade applesauce and home-grown apple pies. The line of forsythia bushes was in bloom.

The oldest Whitey spotted her as she approached the house and waved a red water pistol above his head. "Hi, Miss Trenka! Mom's in the kitchen." And then he was off to creep up on his brothers in some sort of ambush.

Betty didn't care for the idea of guns, even obviously fake ones, in the hands of children.

The scent of turpentine mixed with the smell of baking cookies greeted her as she approached the back door and knocked, although she and Penny seldom stood on cere-mony when visiting.

"Come right in, Betty," Penny said as she wiped off a slim paintbrush, and pushed a curl of blond hair from her forehead with the back of her hand. "I was just trying to do something with this chair."

The wooden chair was painted glossy white, with a fan-ciful handpainted design on the seat and back.

"It looks as though you have done something," Betty said enthusiastically. "It's charming." Penny beamed. She was as proud of her handicraft abilities as she was of her chocolate chip cookies.

"What are the boys doing home on a school day?"

"Some kind of problem at the school, so yesterday they were told not to come in today," Penny said. "Thank good-ness it's a nice day and they can play outside."

"What kind of problem?" Betty didn't really care to know, but she did pay good tax dollars to give the town's kids an education.

"One of the children came down with something that somebody thought might be serious and contagious, so they decided to shut the school for the day."

Betty was glad to know that the boys Brad and Raven mentioned probably weren't cutting school after all.

"Are the school people worried?"

Penny wrinkled her cute little nose. "I don't think so. They said it was just a precaution so the state health people could have a look. They'll all be back at their desks tomorrow, and thank goodness none of mine seems to be showing signs of anything but extreme noisiness." She put her paintbrushes away in a neat wooden box and stood up. "Time to take the cookies out. You'll have coffee, won't you? And a nice chocolate chipper?"

So Betty enjoyed a comfortable cup of coffee and a cookie, and told Penny about her gardening plans.

"Wonderful! You'll get so much enjoyment seeing things grow! I know I do. Oh, and I can share what I've learned in my flower arranging class. What fun we'll have!"

Betty's flower arranging philosophy was first to find some kind of vase and then to cram the flowers into it. She had a momentary flashback to another Martha Stewart Moment that involved skewering stems with florist's wire and wrapping the stems with tape. She brushed that aside as too labor-intensive for her taste, and brought up the matter of her lawn and Penny's nephew. "Ted suggested him."

Penny's sunny smile faded and she frowned. "Tommy's

at the age when he should be doing chores and earning a little money. He's just turned fourteen. Linda finds him a bit of a handful."

She thought for a while as if wondering if Betty was an appropriate person to discuss child-rearing problems with. Then she said, "According to Linda, he's very shy at times, and, well, kind of socially backward. And then he'll start acting up at school and even at home, angry outbursts and swearing, that kind of thing. She feels helpless to deal with it. Since his dad and Linda got divorced, Tommy's been just plain difficult. The divorce hit him hard. We don't have a lot of that in East Moulton, so he's kind of ashamed of it, if you ask me. And I think it's bad for a boy to grow up without a man around—not that Joe ignores him, but it's not the same as having Dad come home every night for dinner and hang out on weekends. Linda worries about the kid all the time. His grades have gone down, and he doesn't have many friends. He just coops himself up in his room to listen to music and play video games. He used to be in the school band, but he dropped out. He used to ride his bike out here from town all the time. He used to get along well with the Whiteys, even if they are just little kids compared to him, but we almost never see him now."

" 'Used to' seems to be a recurring phrase," Betty said.

"That's Tommy. We remember the kid he was. Used to be. Maybe he decided that the Whiteys really were too young for him. And . . ." She hesitated. "He was a real out-going kid, at least around family, but now he's kind of withdrawn and glum. Linda says he's made arguing with her into a fine art. He resents everything she does to give herself a life. He refuses to obey her. I wish I could help, but Greg says it's just a teenage phase he's going through. Look, I'll call Linda and ask her if he'd like to work for you. I know he'd be glad for the money. Linda doesn't make much. I think I told you she works at the dress shop in town and doesn't even get sales commissions. Joe isn't always prompt about sending support money."

Penny was quiet again for a while, fussing with her paintbrushes, carrying Betty's empty coffee mug to the pot for a refill. Then she said, "The divorce was really unfriendly. The *marriage* wasn't all that friendly. He was kind of mean to her." Penny frowned. "I probably shouldn't be telling you this, but I think he used to hurt her sometimes. Maybe Tommy, too."

Sometimes? Betty thought. Once was more than enough as far as she was concerned.

"He remarried soon after they divorced," Penny went on as though she hadn't just said something quite appalling. "Of course, he blamed the split squarely on Linda, he'd never forgive her, blah, blah, but he was the one who was running around. She stayed loyal to him, in spite of everything, right to the end. The new wife has a couple of kids of her own, so I guess finances are tight. The wife hates the idea that he has to give Linda anything."

"Let me know if Tommy is willing to work for me." Betty cringed at further conversation about abusive marriages and hostile divorces. "I'm going to run up to Miho's place and see what kind of flowers she has for planting. The grass can wait for a few days. Anyhow, I can probably arrange with Ted's helper Brad Melville to do it if Tommy can't or won't."

"Don't do it. I don't like him," Penny said firmly.

"Who?"

"Brad. Those creepy eyes of his give me the shivers, and everybody in town says he's nothing but trouble. Some even blame him for all the bad stuff that's been happening, but Tommy thinks he's terrific because he tells a lot of big stories, like how he once had to kill a man with his bare hands. Tommy and a lot of the other kids of that age spend a lot of time hanging out with Brad. What a grown man sees in a pack of boys, I don't know. I keep my boys away from him."

"What sort of 'bad stuff'?" Betty hadn't heard about any "bad stuff" in East Moulton.

"Haven't you heard? There have been some robberies over at that new housing development near the highway. Three or four. I'm worried that old Judit's grandsons are back in town—they're more likely culprits than Brad, but he has that reputation he carries around from when he lived here as a kid. Ask Molly. She knows all about it. But he's no better than he should be. And that girlfriend of his! People in town have nothing good to say about Raven either."

"Like what?" Betty was mildly curious, although she wasn't an indefatigable gossip the way half the town seemed to be. But maybe she would check in with Molly Perkins.

"Oh, the usual rumors about being somewhat too sexually active for the local taste, the way she dresses, the way she talks, just the fact that she lives with Brad without being married to him. Somebody said she's supposed to be a witch. Can you imagine? Our old ladies can dream up the damnedest things."

Betty remembered Raven's—and Brad's—apparent

mind-reading abilities. So she was psychic perhaps, if not an actual witch.

"Miho's orchards will be looking lovely," Penny was saying. "All those gorgeous apple blossoms with the petals falling like snow. It's a mystery to me why Ted doesn't take his bees up to her place and let them gather their honey and pollen where there's plenty to be had."

"I think Ted likes to stay in his little fortress with everything under his control. He has some kind of fruit trees in bloom, and the bees are just getting to work. I was over at his place this morning, and he claims his bees are happy as can be."

"How can you tell anything about a bee's mood?"

To that unanswerable question, Betty shrugged. She stood up. "I'll speak to you later. I'll probably need your advice on how to care for whatever I plant."

"Any time," Penny said. "Give my love to Miho. I hope she's managing okay on her own without her father."

"She's doing all right. She's even enlisted Judit to help her out around the place."

"Judit"—Penny spoke the name awkwardly *you-deet*, the way the old woman pronounced it—"is a funny old duck, isn't she? Lots of talk about her in town, too. The people around here don't care for Gypsies, but at least those boys of hers took off and can't hurt her or anybody now, so I guess they can't really complain about one harmless old lady. But in case they're back, I hope you have a good strong lock on your door. See you later!"

Penny went to pour herself another cup of coffee, but she was looking sober. Perhaps the recollection of her sister's abuse at the hands of her husband and the possible return of Judit's dangerous boys had given her food for thought.

Betty strolled back across the field to her house, wondering if the mild-mannered Greg Saks ever raised his hand to Penny. You never knew what went on in the lives of friends and neighbors. You only saw their smiling faces, and had no idea of the troubles or terrors behind the smiles.

She found Tina waiting on the doorstep, attempting to look pathetic, which was something of a challenge for the hefty animal. "Too early to eat," she said firmly, when she let the cat in and watched her scamper toward the kitchen and the food bowl.

Even in the face of the uncomfortable revelation about Penny's sister's marriage, Betty's optimism remained high. It was a good day, and in spite of Brad and Raven, she still felt that something good was going to happen. It really wasn't so bad to have nothing serious to do, not on a day like this.

What happened was that the phone rang.

And when she'd finished talking, she had a job. Not a long-term one, not one that would make a lot of money, but at least it wasn't a tedious job of typing a résumé for an eager and inexperienced young woman anxious to enter the work force.

Sarah Carlson, the principal of the local school, had offered her the job of school secretary for a few weeks. The regular secretary had taken ill suddenly, although it had nothing to do with the health scare that had closed the school for today.

"The town librarian recommended you," Sarah Carlson

said, "and my son is part of that reading group at the library, so he knows you."

"Donnie Carlson is your boy?"

Mrs. Carlson laughed. "Even principals have children, Miss Trenka. Although it's not easy on the kid, being a member of the boss's family. I understand you've had quite a bit of office experience, and the people in town speak highly of you. If you don't mind children and can do the necessary routine tasks, we'd like to have you. Mrs. Thurlow isn't likely to be out sick for very long, but we're coming to the end of the school year and there are a number of things that have to get done. Normally we'd follow more complicated hiring procedures that involve the school board, but I don't want Ellen to feel that we're taking her job away, so if we take you on as a temp, so to speak, she's more likely to rest easy and get well sooner. Can you do it?"

"I certainly can," Betty said. "I don't mind children, although I haven't had a lot of experience with them. When do you want me?"

"Is tomorrow morning too soon?"

"Fine," Betty said. "Ummm, do I need to get shots for whatever is going around the school?"

"No, no, and I don't want you to worry about that. The health people don't think there's a problem, only one boy got sick, and it was probably something he ate."

"What time does school start? Eight-thirty? I'll be there well before then."

Betty replaced the receiver and smiled broadly.

Something good had happened after all, just as she had imagined it would. She was going back to work and could laugh—at least for a while—at her enforced retirement.

When Sid Edwards Junior had decided that both she and his father, Sid Senior, were too old to continue at Edwards & Son and had made them retire, she'd seen the future looming empty and bleak. Edwards & Son had been all she'd known for more than three decades. Even after she'd left Hartford to move south to East Moulton, she hadn't been able to find a focus for her life. Planting a few petunias in her backyard wasn't what she had in mind.

But now she had a job, for a few weeks at least.

The wretched lawn could grow to its heart's content, for all she cared. She had a job.

It was only later that she remembered Raven's words about finding her place, and now she had and she was at peace. Then she wondered if the rest would come true as well, and she would find herself tumbling off the thin edge into unexpected turmoil.

One thing she was sure of. She didn't wish to encounter either Raven or Brad Melville again soon.

CHAPTER 4

THE DAY was half over and she was going to go to work tomorrow. What to do now? Look over her clothes, of course, so she'd appear suitably serious and professional, although she suspected that little kids didn't really know much about women's clothes. Then she remembered that the school included not only elementary grades and the middle school, but the high school as well. She would be dealing with children of all ages. A terrifying thought. Not just the boisterous Whiteys of East Moulton but knowing, sophisticated teenagers too. The high schoolers would certainly be fashion-conscious, but maybe not too critical of a woman they would view as elderly. Well, she still had the clothes that she used to wear when she was working for Edwards & Son, and they would have to do. Her plans to pay a visit to Miho? She could still work that in, and this afternoon she could plant what she bought. How long could it take? Not long at all, if she could manage to dissuade Judit from reading her cards.

It looked to be a full day, after all, and she felt that her early optimism hadn't been misplaced.

The sky continued to be cloudless and bright, a clear, pure blue; the air smelled so good that she wanted to fill a glass with it and drink it down. Her trusty Buick seemed to have spring in its gas tank, because it flew along (too fast, probably, for Timberhill Road, but that was Betty's fault rather than the car's) until she reached Main Street. The doors to all the shops were open, and the shopkeepers and salespersons hovered in the doorways to catch a bit of the glorious day. Quite a number of children were skating and biking along the sidewalks, enjoying their day off from boring lessons and enclosed classrooms.

Suddenly Betty pulled the Buick over to the side of the road and turned off the engine. She was in front of Town & Country Fashions, a small, square building detached from its neighbors, with two big display windows filled with elegantly posed mannequins wearing soft pastel dresses. Since it was the only dress shop in East Moulton, it must be the place where Penny's sister Linda worked. She could ask now about hiring Tommy as her lawn boy. Besides, there might be a frock here she could buy for her new job.

The store was dim after the bright sunshine outside. Betty didn't immediately see any other customers, or indeed any sales help. Then she heard a wild shriek of laughter from the back of the shop, and peered past the racks of dresses, slacks, and blouses in the direction of the sound.

Now she caught sight of a slim young woman who seemed to be a salesperson, who was handing a bright pink garment through the curtain of a dressing room.

"It can't look that hysterical," Betty heard her say.

"Pink! On me! Can you imagine it?" said a voice from the dressing room. Betty edged closer. And the closer she got, the more the young saleswoman reminded her of

Penny. It certainly must be Linda, Penny's sister. Betty now recalled her from their one brief meeting. Like Tommy, Linda didn't seem to visit the Saks house often, or Betty would have seen more of her.

"Now, Raven, don't reject it so quickly. It's a beautiful dress," Linda said, and Betty froze. She didn't care to encounter Raven for the second time in one day, and she started to back away toward the door. Then Linda looked around and caught sight of her. "Can I help you, ma'am? Oh, it's Miss Trenka. I'm Penny Saks's sister, Linda. We met when you first moved here. Penny talks about you all the time."

"Doesn't this damn store have *anything* in black?" In the dressing room, Raven had had enough of pink.

"Just a minute, dear. I think there's a black silk shirtwaist in your size." Linda rolled her eyes as if to say to Betty, These girls, and this one especially.

"Don't patronize me with your 'dears,' " Raven almost shouted, "save it for your boyfriend." Then she added petulantly, "I don't like dresses, you know that. I like pants, shirts, simple stuff." She emerged from the dressing room clad only in a long black T-shirt that reached to her thighs. She was barefoot, and her toenails were as red as her fingernails. There was no sign of the pink garment that had inspired her laughter. "Well, it's Miss Trenka. Are you following me?"

"Not at all," Betty said. "I was just . . . looking for something to wear to work."

"Where's that man-stealing Linda got to?" Raven tossed her long hair impatiently. "Ah, there she is."

Betty was mystified. She didn't think from the looks of

Linda that she was the type to steal the likes of Brad Melville. She shrugged mentally. No accounting for taste.

Linda was working her way through a rack of dresses until she pulled a soft, floating black silk dress from the bar and held it up to her body to show it to Raven. "What do you think? It's tailored, no hilarious ruffles, no pink, but still soft and feminine. You could wear it everywhere."

Raven shrugged. "I don't go everywhere, and I'm not soft and feminine, but what the hell, I'll try it on." She snatched it from Linda and returned to the dressing room.

"Raven has her own sense of style, but I think she's not sure of it," Linda said. "Odd girl. My boy Tommy is fond of her, which is odd, too, since he's not much of one for women of any age or style, although he has been talking about some girl at school that he 'likes,' whatever that means to a fourteen-year-old. And speaking of liking, Raven definitely doesn't like me. I'm not a man-stealer, and she hates it that I sometimes forbid Tommy to go about with her and Brad."

"Ah, Linda, I was talking to Penny about Tommy this morning." Betty caught a flicker of anxiety on Linda's face as she spoke.

"What's he done now? Honestly, that boy."

"Why nothing, nothing at all." Now she definitely had to discuss the lawn job, lest Linda think her sister gossiped with a stranger about Tommy's problems. "I'm looking for someone to mow my lawn this summer. It's a little too much for me, and Ted Kelso, our neighbor across the road, suggested Tommy, so I asked Penny to ask you if he'd like to do it this spring and summer. But since I'm here, I'm asking you myself. He'd be right next door to the Whiteys and his aunt."

She could see Linda relax, now that Tommy wasn't involved in some trouble. "I'll certainly ask him," Linda said. "He's really a good boy, Miss Trenka, just a little rambunctious, except of course when he decides to become shy and difficult. How does that dress look, Raven?" she called out. "Let us see you in it."

After a moment, the dressing room curtain was flung aside and Raven glided out, looking nearly normal, even beautiful. Black really did suit her, Betty decided. She'd taken the time to pin up her hair and put on a pair of long silver earrings along with the silver pendant at her throat. Her waist was noticeably tiny in the belted dress with its wide flowing skirt, and the bare feet gave her a girlish look.

"How lovely," Linda said. "It's perfect on you."

Raven made a face. "It's not bad, but Brad will tell me I've sold my soul to the fashion devil. Our friend Phil is a sucker for this kind of proper-lady stuff." Linda frowned briefly. Then Raven shrugged and smiled, "But I've done worse. I do like it, more than I ever thought I'd like a dress." She rubbed the silken fabric on the arms of the dress, which had wide sleeves gathered with elastic at the wrists so they billowed gracefully. "I'll take it."

"Of course you will," Linda said.

"What do you think, Miss Trenka? Do I look like a femme fatale? Or maybe just bewitching?" She laughed a throaty laugh and admired herself in a mirror.

"You look very nice, Raven," Betty said. "Are you going to a party?"

"Not a party exactly, but we do have our events. May Day is coming up, you know, and sometimes it pays to look better than the rest of the time," Raven said. She went back into the dressing room to change. Betty examined some blouses that might go with the simple skirts and jackets left over from her Edwards & Son days.

"I'm going to be working at the school for a few weeks," Betty said. "The secretary's ill."

"I heard about Ellen Thurlow," Linda said. "A kidney infection, from what Molly Perkins says. I hope it's not serious; she's a nice woman. Well, you'll be seeing Tommy there." She laughed a bit bitterly. "He's always getting sent to the principal's office. Some people tell me he's hyperactive. You couldn't tell that from the way he is at home. Quiet as can be, sort of sulky, always in his room, playing his video games, getting on the Internet, all that stuff I don't really understand. And if I say no to anything at all, he flies into a perfect rage."

"I don't understand all that cyberspace stuff myself," Betty said, avoiding the question of Tommy's rages. She selected three blouses, put two back and kept the one with the tiny flower print. The she tried on a light blue linen blazer.

"Nice," Linda said. "Perfect for the school office, or maybe the navy would be better. Schools are grubby places, and the light blue might get soiled."

"Wrap up the dress," Raven said. She was back to her usual jeans and T-shirt. She fished out a rather large roll of bills from her big black shoulder bag. "You tell Tommy that Brad and I expect to see him tomorrow night with the rest of the gang."

"Tomorrow is Wednesday, and that's a school night," Linda said. "I don't think I can allow him to go out. . . ."

"It'll be over early." Raven sounded bored with Linda's motherly concern. "We're getting together at six, and will be finished by seven. Brad found a bunch of pictures he took in North Africa. The boys are dying to see them. Camels and stuff. You know how kids are."

"We'll see," Linda said. She narrowed her eyes.

"I'll take the light blue," Betty said. She had her own stubborn streak, and after all, she wasn't going to be working at the school forever. And she liked the light blue. "And this blouse."

"The customer is always right," Linda said.

"I was sure right about the pink dress," Raven said. "It made my skin look . . . funny. Black is still best." She picked up the box holding her dress and glided out of the shop. "You take care now, Miss Trenka. Lots of crazy drivers on the road."

"What a strange person," Betty said, and then she fleetingly worried about a crazed driver smashing into the Buick, just because Raven had mentioned it.

Linda frowned. "Stranger than you think. And dangerous, too, I imagine. Well, here are your things, and I'll speak to Tommy about the mowing as soon as I get home. It would be good for him to have a real responsibility. He won't do much at home. And if he fails you, I'll come over and do it myself."

"Why would he fail? And, Linda, why would he be spending time with the likes of Raven and Brad? Not just the adventure stories, but really."

"All the kids do. Despite everything, Raven and Brad are really good with the boys. I don't have a lot of time for him, and I think it's nice for Tommy to have a role model . . . an older guy like Brad." Betty's expression conveyed her doubt that Brad was much of a role model, so Linda changed gears quickly. "It's just kids having fun, dreaming about the kind of adventures Brad has had, and Brad's a guy, a man Tommy can bond with. Since his father left us, he hasn't had anybody like that.

"I'm seeing someone now, a nice person, but Phil and Tommy don't get along too well. Phil's one of those guys who likes to take charge—not that he means any harm, but Tommy resents being told what to do by somebody who's not his father." She looked Betty in the eye. "Then there's Raven. She's kind of possessive about Phil, an old friend, and she's trying to punish me by making Tommy prefer her company to mine. Do you understand kids? I don't." Suddenly the perky blond woman became a defeated child. "I don't understand *me*, let alone a teenager. I tried so hard to save my marriage, but no. The grass was a lot greener to Joe in that tramp's yard. Tommy's the one who's suffered most. He hated the fights, and he hated it when Joe left. Joe didn't really mean to hurt me, but he knew what he was doing. He sort of forgot that there are hurts other than bruises, especially when there's a kid involved." Linda looked at Betty desperately. "Please don't say a word to Penny. Joe never touched Tommy. Really. He was strict but he never hit him. Why am I telling you this?" She sighed. "It's that Raven. She can come swanning in here like Queen of the Universe and make me feel like I know zip. I work here all day, rush home to make dinner for Tommy and see that he does his homework, get him to bed, wake up, get him to school, and still try to have a little time for me." The pain of her life was obvious.

"It will all work out," Betty said with false cheerfulness, and quickly took her purchases and departed. Somehow a cloud had passed across the jubilant spring sky and dimmed the bright day.

Don't interfere, she told herself sternly, and it's still a beautiful day, no matter how sad Linda thinks her life is.

She got into the car and eased out into the almost nonexistent traffic, but before she headed toward Miho's greenhouses on the road out of town, she decided to stop at the pharmacy for a brief chat with Molly.

"Betty, Betty, it's been ages since I've seen you." Molly's bright eyes looked her over for signs of something she could share with her fellow gossips. "You're looking very well. It must be this wonderful weather. I hear you're to work at the school while poor Ellen recovers. What a blessing they had someone right here in town to help Sarah. That poor woman works night and day keeping all those children in order."

"I'm looking forward to it," Betty said. "I like keeping busy. Umm, Molly, people have been talking about Brad Melville. . . ."

Molly sniffed her disapproval. "That one. I've known him since he was a boy, and I couldn't believe that he'd dare to show his face again in East Moulton, not after what he did."

Betty waited, then said, "What did he do?"

"You must know, everybody does." Molly was appalled by Betty's lack of knowledge of the town's history, at least the sordid parts. "Well, maybe you wouldn't have heard, since you've only been here a short time."

Betty didn't have to wait long to hear.

"The Melvilles moved to East Moulton about twenty years ago; Brad was six or seven. Cute little boy, although even then he had those eyes of his. Jasper Melville was an electrician. Did a good business, everyone said, when he showed up to work, but he was a drunk and unreliable, and that's what people remember. Mean and bad when he drank. I remember the time he got into a fight with Everett over at the gas station about something Jasper was supposed to do and didn't. Bloody mess it was, with Jasper coming out the worst. Swore he'd fix Everett good."

"And did he?"

"Well, the town kind of turned against him, because Everett was a real pillar of the community, and the fellows around the garage when it happened said Jasper started it, so the Melvilles were kind of ostracized. Jasper's business fell off to nothing. Then Everett's gas station burned down, big explosion and everything. A few people were injured, but Everett died. He was working there late, keeping the place open. That got people really worked up. They blamed Jasper. It's that empty lot at the end of Main Street. Nothing ever got built there after the fire."

"The place that's used as a parking lot now? I always wondered why nothing was there. And did Jasper do it? Set the fire?"

"Not him. He was home dead drunk that night, if you can believe Mary Melville, and I do. No, people started saying that it was Brad who did it. He was fourteen, fifteen at the time, ran around with a pack of bad boys. Nothing was ever proved, but from that time on, the Melvilles had a bad time of it here. Then the boy started talking about getting even with the town for ruining their lives. He was mixed up in pranks—paint splashed on houses, mailboxes knocked over, a couple of break-ins just to mess up someone's house, not to steal anything. It got so nobody would speak to Mary when she went to the market or Jasper when he ate at the diner. Then Jasper died of the drink, and Mary packed up Brad and they moved away.

Good riddance. I suppose he's come back now to get even, since he couldn't do it when he was a kid."

"I don't see how he's getting even now," Betty said. "Unless seducing the kids with his tales is getting revenge."

"He's brought that tart here, and if she's setting a good example to our young ladies, then I'm a chicken with two heads. And you've heard about the recent robberies, haven't you? If you ask me, they've got Brad Melville's fingerprints all over them, no matter what the constable and Officer Bob say. He's going to turn those boys into wild things, criminals, and nobody's going to be safe in their beds. I hope they run him out of town again." Molly was on a roll, and Betty thought that nothing she might say would change her mind. Still, she tried.

"If nothing's been proved, he can't be guilty of anything. Surely they brought in arson investigators when that fire happened. . . ."

"Oh, he's guilty all right. He's always been too smart to get caught. Probably learned all the tricks in those outlandish places he says he's traveled to."

Elizabeth Trenka certainly wasn't going to change Molly's mind about anything, so she bought some sunscreen to protect her when she attempted to garden, and went on her way to Miho's place. Main Street in East Moulton was slumbering in the midday sun, and even the kids had departed to play at home in the shade.

At the four-way stop sign where she had to turn left for the road to Miho's greenhouse and farm, a car coming from the opposite direction failed to come to a full stop, and Betty had to slam on her brakes in the middle of the intersection. Score another point for Raven and her psychic powers.

She waited in the intersection for a moment to regain her tranquillity, to allow the other car to move ahead, and to give her beating heart a chance to get back to normal. And to convince herself that the driver of the other car was not Brad Melville. No, certainly not.

But the other driver waved a sort of apology, and she thought she saw those marble and onyx eyes.

CHAPTER 5

AFTER SHE managed to calm down, it was a pleasure to drive slowly along the country road away from East Moulton center toward Miho's place, and to forget about Raven in her new black dress, and poor Linda raising her son alone while trying to create some sort of life for herself. Then she couldn't help but think about Raven's words—"man-stealer" with some man's name mentioned—and the conflict between the two women over Tommy's involvement with Brad. Which brought her back to dangerous drivers at intersections, possibly predicted by Raven. It was all too much.

Betty concentrated on the road and the explosion of spring along the roadside. Before long, she could see the start of the apple orchards on Miho's property. The trees were indeed already a mass of pink and white blossoms. She even thought she could smell their sweetness on the breeze that flowed in through the open windows of the car. Soon she was pulling into the dirt area in front of the greenhouse and the neat white house Miho had once shared with her late father and an admittedly difficult husband.

The wooden produce stand was in place, but the shelves

were bare of squashes and tomatoes and green bouquets of broccoli. It was of course far too early for even the earliest vegetables. However, there were several flats of seedlings on the stand, tiny yellow marigolds, some blue flowers, as well as petunias in pink, white, and purple, lots of pansies, and a few other flowering plants she didn't recognize. That wasn't surprising. Martha Stewart's floral fantasies ran to fat hydrangeas twisted into huge wreaths and exotic roses made into bridal bouquets, mosses tucked into crevices of stone walls, and giant ferns designed for rain forests. Betty only knew what Martha told her, and she didn't recall a single pansy. The greenhouse, of course, was filled with orchids, Miho's great love, but Betty had no idea about orchid life cycles, and whether they were aroused to special blooming brilliance by the springtime. She rather thought not, as they seemed to be self-centered plants that existed mainly to be admired.

Before she went to find Miho, who was probably baby-ing her treasures in the greenhouse, she caught sight of Judit's disreputable-looking RV parked on a flat stretch of ground on the other side of the house. Judit had made her-self quite at home. There was a clothesline strung between an apple tree and a maple with a couple of ruffled skirts and a blue denim work shirt hanging from it. Nearby was a circle of rocks that looked like a makeshift campfire with a beat-up folding chaise beside it. Judit was nowhere to be seen, but the doors of the RV were open. Betty ap-proached, mindful of Brad's comment about "the old woman" and "pain."

"Ooo-hoo! Judit!" she called.

"Elizabeth . . ." The voice was faint and came from the RV. Like Ted, Judit was careful to call Betty by her preferred name. For that alone, she ranked high on Betty's list of preferred people.

Betty peered in through the door into musty dimness.

She could make out a heap of clothes and old quilts on a cot. The pile suddenly moved, and Judit struggled to sit upright. Her unlikely red hair was tousled and she seemed to be wearing a vast white nightshirt, but her ropes of gold necklaces were around her neck, and gold hoops dangled from her ears.

"An evil day," Judit said. "Evil is abroad." She groaned slightly.

"Whatever is the matter?" Betty asked. "Are you ill?"

"I have a pain," Judit said. "It comes from being old. You are as old as I am. You understand pain."

Betty didn't really, because except for a few aching joints, she never felt much pain of any kind. She didn't even have headaches. However, she didn't care to argue with Judit. "I think I have some aspirin with me, will they help?" Molly at the pharmacy had persuaded her to buy a little pocket dispenser of aspirin "just in case."

"Little pills won't take away the pain that comes from evil," Judit said as though she was explaining a momentous fact of life to a backward child. But she held out her hand, and Betty rummaged through her handbag to find the aspirin.

She wondered again how Brad could have known about Judit's pain as she dropped two tablets into the pudgy outstretched hand. Judit popped them into her mouth and reached for a mug on the floor beside the cot.

"I came to see Miho about buying some plants," Betty said, "but if there's anything I can do for you . . . Maybe if you tell me where the pain is? Or have you told Miho? She used to be a nurse."

Judit waved her away and lay back on the cot. "The Japanese girl and I do not talk much. She brings me tea," she said, "and some kind of awful sticky rice with pieces of fish. I like big stews with meat and potatoes. That's what I used to cook for my husband and children, but at least I'm not starving. The other girl brings me better things to eat."

"Other girl?"

"The one who thinks she's a witch with the key to all the secrets of life. She tells me she is studying the old secrets and will soon master them." Judit's cackle indicated that she didn't believe any of it for a second. "But she does looks like a witch, all black and nasty."

"Is she called Raven?"

"She is like a big, black bird with red claws," Judit said. "She asks me questions because she thinks I know something of value. But even if I could answer her with what she wants to know, I will not tell her. My people have knowledge learned from centuries of hard experience, from thousands of miles along hard, slow roads. She wants to pick up bits of wisdom like you pick up fallen apples. She does not want to work for it. And if she had my knowledge, she would use it wrong. Already she's a bad 'un, she is."

"A bad witch?"

Another cackle from the cot. "She's not a witch. I don't think there are such things, not anymore. The old ones have died off, and there are none to replace them. This ugly black bird plays at it. I told you, she has no knowledge, no training. Maybe she has read a book, or talked to people who claim to know such things. But she's not looking for magic potions and spells. What she wants is power, ways to control others, to keep them bent to her will. Most of all, I think she wants money, because she knows that's the way to true power."

"Do you know her friend Brad?"

"Another bad 'un. He says he knows my grandsons, he met them on the road, but I do not know if I believe him." Judit shook her head sadly. "The boys are gone, and they would only come back if there's something in it for them." She grinned at Betty. "But I think they would like that black girl and her red nails.

"The boy who is with the black girl talks about magic, too, but men don't have the right equipment in their brains for that. It's power they want, but a different kind from what a woman wants. My boys . . ." She was still talking about the grandsons who had threatened and abandoned her. ". . . they know the only power they have is in their muscles. Smart boys in that at least." She groaned again. "I wish this pain would go away."

"When did you see Brad and Raven?"

"Yesterday, the day before . . . I don't pay attention to the days at my age. I pay attention to the pain, and I hide from the evil of the day."

So Brad could easily have known that Judit was not feeling well, simply from speaking to her. It was a relief to know that he wasn't a mind reader, merely an opportunist. It was even possible that Judit had mentioned her friend Betty Trenka when Brad was here.

"Did you mention me to Brad and Raven?"

"Who knows what I said? It's all empty noise, talking is. The only true voice comes from the cards."

"I really must see Miho. I have a lot to do," Betty said quickly. She definitely didn't want Judit to bring out her pack of bent fortune-telling cards. She'd had enough of dire predictions, and she didn't want more to spoil her still optimistic mood. Then she felt she had to share her news. "I'm going to work tomorrow, Judit. I got a job. Just for a few weeks, but it will be wonderful to get back to doing something with a purpose."

"Humph, jobs. A woman doesn't need a job. A woman is born with work to do. She cooks and cleans and washes the clothes for her husband and sons."

"Have neither, never had them, don't need them now," Betty said. "But I'll call Miho in a day or two to see how you're feeling. Be sure to have her call me if the pain gets worse. And if you like, I'll take you to a doctor."

"Don't like doctors," Judit said stubbornly. "My people never go to doctors. But you are good to offer. I knew from the first that you were my friend, Elizabeth." Judit contrived to sound weak and frail, rather like the sturdy Tina attempting to appear undernourished and pathetic, but she had a contented little smile, so Betty felt she wasn't suffering greatly at the moment.

Miho was in the greenhouse, dressed in her usual smock, baggy pants, and thick sandals. She was cooing over an orchid that didn't look like much to Betty, but then, Betty couldn't tell a thousand-dollar orchid from a fancy weed.

"Hello, Miho. Judit seems to be all right, so now I need some plants to put in my garden."

"Ah, Miss Trenka. You can choose from the ones already outside, but if they don't please you, I have more that will be ready for planting in a week or two. I don't believe it will turn cold again, and I feel that spring is truly here."

"I'm not fussy," Betty said, "and I shall be surprised if they don't die as soon as I put them in the ground, no matter what the temperature. Miho, is Judit any trouble to you?"

Miho smiled. "She is an old lady, who grumbles and complains, but she stays to herself. I brought her food when she was not feeling well, but she is much improved. She makes a little fire outside in the evenings. Sometimes I hear her singing. She washes some clothes, and she has helped me with looking after the vegetables that I have just begun to plant. She pulls weeds and turns the hose on the little sprouts. And she will be more help when the crops grow bigger. No, she is no trouble."

"Have her boys been back since they left town?"

"I have not seen them," Miho said, "but one boy from town has been here."

"Brad Melville. With his girlfriend Raven."

"I don't like them," Miho said. "The girl squeals about my beautiful orchids, but I won't give one to her as she wishes. I won't even let her buy one. She says they look as though they come from outer space, and that insults them, so I tell her that I have chores to do, and I lock the greenhouse so she won't steal any. I think she would steal if the door was open. The boy is a friend of Ted's, so I do not chase them away, although I don't understand why they wish to talk to the old woman."

"Maybe she reads their cards," Betty said.

Miho shook her head. "That is nonsense, thinking the cards can tell you what your life will be. I think they bring her rum and that is why I hear her singing in the night. If my father were still alive, he would probably like to sit by the fire with her and talk, although he spoke only Japanese, and she often talks to herself in her own language." She smiled at the thought of an old Japanese orchid grower chatting in Japanese with an old Eastern European refugee loaded down with gold necklaces and sporting dyed red hair. "She is harmless, but I think she can be fierce, so I am glad to have someone about now that I am all alone." She thought for a moment. "Brad did promise that he would send boys to help pick the apples in my orchard in the fall, and gather the vegetables in the summer. That will be good. I said I would pay them." For a moment she looked troubled. "But I am afraid he will take the money and not give any to his helpers. He does not like our town; he said it killed his father. He speaks of revenge."

Betty wondered whether Brad's boys always did their little jobs about town with Brad receiving the payment. Nice scam, a way for him to get money without exerting himself. Taking the boys' hard-earned money would be another way to get even with the town he hated. Then she wondered if what she paid Tommy to mow her lawn would end up in Brad's pocket.

"I don't trust him much," Betty said. "Based on nothing, but still . . ." It was time for her to get home, do her planting, and think about getting ready to appear at the school in the morning. She selected a flat of yellow marigolds, some bright-faced pansies, and pink petunias.

"If you come back later, there will be the other flowers," Miho said. "You can plant them anytime now that the weather is staying warm. Once you start to enjoy seeing things grow, you will want more and more, and then you will want rare plants to see if you can make them grow too, and you will start trying to grow flowers from seeds. Then you will decide that you must plant tomatoes and peas and little lettuces because they are so good to eat. It is like an addiction. You'll see. But no orchids." She grinned. "They are more expensive than children."

"If you say so," Betty said. She was already beginning to have doubts about both her skill and continuing enthusiasm as a gardener. It had seemed like such a good idea that morning. But never let it be said that Elizabeth Trenka gave up on anything she was determined to do. And she always tried to do it to the best of her ability.

She loaded the plants in the trunk of her car, and looked back at Miho standing in the door of her greenhouse with her precious orchids stretched out behind her. She had been about to ask Miho if she ever sensed that a day was evil the way Judit did. Then she remembered that evil had visited Miho not long before in the cold snowy days of winter, and decided to keep silent.

It wasn't long before Betty was on her knees in her backyard, with a trowel she'd found in the basement and even a battered old watering can, digging new homes for her frail little seedlings. She put the pink petunias together in a bunch and edged the strip of earth with the yellow marigolds. The pansies seemed to be smiling up at her from their cozy bed.

All right, she told herself, you're not artistic, you're just a beginner. Then she had a picture of a tall row of black-eyed Susans along the back of the garden, and stately sweetpeas, the way her mother used to plant them. She wondered if the plant addiction was beginning to take hold, as Miho had suggested it would. As she looked about the yard for a place for the compost heap, she thought that Martha Stewart would be proud of her.

She watered the plants, and by the time the afternoon was drawing to a close, she was fairly well satisfied with her work. Her nails were caked with dirt. She'd have to do something about that before she reached the school in the morning.

She was scrubbing her nails at the kitchen sink as twilight deepened in the backyard so that she could only dimly see the row of yellow marigolds and spots of white on the pansies' faces, when she caught sight of a person moving through the yard.

She hesitated and then relaxed. It was a boy pushing a bicycle. It was a blond boy, slight and not too tall. His looks immediately reminded her of the towheaded Whitey Sakses next door. This might well be their cousin Tommy, here to see about the mowing job.

She opened the back door, but the boy hung back. "Leave your bike there, it'll be okay," she said. "Are you Tommy?"

"Yes, ma'am. My mom said I should come. . . ."

"Come on in, and we'll talk business," Betty said.

Tommy edged into the kitchen, his head down, and stood awkwardly in the middle of the room. He was, of course, much shorter than Betty, who towered over almost everyone, and his hair flopped around his ears and brushed the neck of his T-shirt. Perhaps he was trying to grow it long like Brad's. He didn't seem eager to meet her eye, and he fidgeted without saying anything.

"Would you like a Coke or something?" Betty hoped it wasn't an idle offer, but she was sure there were a couple of cans of pop in her refrigerator.

"Nope. I'm okay. Mom said you wanted someone to mow your lawn. Brad said it would be okay to do it."

"So you take your advice from Brad?" Betty was curious.

"Gee, sure. He knows what to do and all kinds of stuff." Suddenly Tommy was a bit more animated, and now he did look her in the eye, but Betty wasn't encouraged by what she saw. His eyes seemed unfocused, simply empty pools of pale blue as though there was nothing there, no feelings except sadness, no eager, boyish thoughts of how he might spend his earnings.

"Stuff?" she said quickly.

"You know, like when to work, when to play, when to get even when they treat you bad. He's been like, everywhere, Europe, Africa, and India and places like that. He's been in fights and he always wins. He even killed a guy once, he told us all about it. They were after him, and he had to get away." Tommy was becoming more animated by the minute. "He works out, so he's real strong, not just muscles but in his mind. Power is what's important, he says. He's teaching me to be powerful so I don't get beat down by anybody. Not anymore. People will have to be real nice to me, because I'll have all the power."

Betty didn't like the sudden, feverish excitement in his face and in his voice. No matter how much Tommy needed a man in his life, she didn't think Brad Melville was a good role model for this boy. But it wasn't her business.

"You have to remember, Tommy, that people telling big tales might be doing just that, telling tales. They sometimes make things up so they'll sound important." Lord, hadn't she heard a hundred stories from the salesmen at Edwards & Son about their triumphs, only to learn later that they were never quite the shining moments that had been recounted. She assumed it was a man thing. Comforting fantasy covering the face of unpleasant reality.

"Could you come around on Saturday, morning or afternoon?" she asked. "It doesn't matter which. You'd mow the front lawn and the backyard so it looks nice, trim along the foundations of the house. It shouldn't take too long." She'd have to remember to borrow Ted's mower, but she might have time to get a new one by Saturday. Except that she had a job to consider.

"Is it a power mower?"

"Well, no. Not yet. I may get one later, but it's not a very big yard, not half as big as your aunt Penny's."

Then they settled on a price and Tommy promised to come on Saturday afternoon, because, he told her solemnly, Brad was taking the guys to shoot rats at the town dump in the morning. "They're more active then, Brad says."

Betty held no brief for rats, but the idea was distasteful. Still, boys will be boys, she thought, and if they had to shoot something, it might as well be vermin.

Around eight o'clock that evening, Penny phoned to tell her that she'd talked to Linda, and Tommy had agreed to handle her lawn and that he'd come on Saturday morning.

"He's already been here, and we made a deal for him to come in the afternoon. He had something else to do in the morning," Betty said. She didn't choose to discuss Tommy's plans for hunting rats. "He seems like a nice boy."

"He is. But it's funny that he didn't stop here," Penny said. "He's been known to sample of few of my cookies. Kids—I can't figure them. Did you get your flowers?"

"All safely in the ground. You'll have to come around to see them, if they're not all dead by morning."

"Don't be a pessimist. Flowers like that are easy, so everything will turn out okay."

Then Betty told Penny about her job, but Penny had already heard about it from Linda.

"Sisters do have a right to gossip," Penny said defensively. "I know all about the clothes you bought, and about Raven's appearance at the shop. They don't get along very well because of Tommy." She paused. "How did Linda strike you? Is she doing okay? It's hard for me to tell because she's my sister and she always seems the same to me, no matter what. Even when her husband left her, she didn't seem any different. Well, there were a few tears and a lot of anger. . . . Even if she was well rid of Joe, she was hurt."

"She does seem a bit stressed by her responsibilities, raising Tommy and working, but I have no way of judging," Betty said.

"She's probably okay," Penny said. "I must have been imagining things. I was afraid Joe had been around bothering her. He seems to enjoy popping in and making trouble. Anyhow, I'm glad she's found herself a boyfriend. She won't say much about him, but his name's Phil, and he's a teacher at the school. I wanted to ask Tommy . . ." She stopped and Betty heard an awkward little laugh, as though Penny realized that pumping her nephew for tales about his mother's boyfriend was not really appropriate. Betty remembered that Raven had spoken of someone named Phil at the dress shop, somehow in connection with man-stealing. She waited to hear if Penny had more to offer, but she didn't say anything else, merely wished Betty good luck with her job and invited her to dinner tomorrow evening, so Betty wouldn't have to feed herself after her first day at work.

"I'll probably be a wreck," Betty said. "If you can't figure out kids, think of poor me, who's never had to deal with them."

"Don't worry about them. They'll sit up and take notice if you're in charge. You're kind of . . . of formidable, you know. I'll make spaghetti," Penny said. "The best kind of food after a hard day's work."

Formidable? Betty thought about that. She was tall, she was firm, she didn't look like a pushover, but kids today . . . well, she watched as much television as the next person, and she read the papers. All through her working life at Edwards & Son, she'd managed to handle the young people who worked there without any problems. Of course, she had enough power to make her word law, but . . . Power again. Well, hers was the power of experience and a fairly strong moral sense. And the power of age, of having survived for many decades. What did a third-grader have to match that?

She retired to bed early, with Tina at her feet, feeling that she was well up to the task that lay before her. She didn't dream often, but tonight she had a long, lazy dream that featured a solemn Tommy, trailed by ghostly forms that looked like Brad and Raven . . . but the ground they walked on was a carpet of pansies.

CHAPTER 6

BETTY WAS up before the sun on the first day of her new job. She had always judged the young women she hired at Edwards & Son by their willingness to get to work earlier than "exactly on time," or worse, "just a little late."

It was going to be another fine day, and the children would likely be regretting that they had to return to school after their day off in the sun. Well, even if they were difficult today, she thought the job of a school secretary would not entail much steady interaction with students, no discipline required of her except the power of an adult's presence to dampen high spirits. Still, there were certainly numerous details to be learned about rules and routines. She could handle it.

She wore her new light blue blazer, the new blouse with the flower print, and a navy skirt. Deciding on shoes was a bit of a problem. She'd become so accustomed to wearing sneakers and other sensible shoes in her retirement that she didn't have much to choose from. Then she found the low-heeled navy pumps she used to wear to work. They needed a bit of polishing but would be entirely suitable. She could always buy new shoes. Then she remembered that this job wasn't for a lifetime, only a few weeks until Ellen Thurlow recovered.

Tina didn't seem too downcast by Betty's early morning bustling. However, she did eye the full dish of dry cat food with some dismay. She preferred tuna.

"You'll be glad of it when I'm not around all day to cater to your every whim," Betty said. "And you'll miss not having me to kick around." Tina condescended to nibble at the dry food, and even went so far as to bat a nugget around the kitchen floor in an uncharacteristically playful manner. Betty understood cats less than she understood children.

The school wasn't far away, just off Main Street near East Moulton center, a matter of a five-minute drive. She managed to arrive at eight, with half an hour to spare before the start of the school day. Yellow school buses were already disgorging bunches of students, ranging from first-graders to high schoolers. They divided themselves into separate streams to enter the school. It was an ugly, hulking, old-fashioned redbrick structure, like the school she'd attended many decades ago, only then it had probably been almost new. Attached to the East Moulton school was a modern one-story addition stretching away to the right, all glass windows and pale stone. The youngest children seemed to be heading for the new building, while the teens bounded up the steps of the old one.

The parking lot was on the left side, with a few cars already there. Groups of teens clustered at the end of the lot near a bicycle rack. A few unteacherlike cars indicated that some of the older students probably had their own cars. Betty decided that the front part of the lot, near the main entrance, would logically be reserved for teachers and staff. She picked a place, and hoped she wasn't going to offend someone who regularly parked in that space. Nothing to be done about that now. She hoped, too, that Sarah Carlson got to school early, so she could ask some questions before the day began.

The building was not warm or welcoming, and the date above the door read 1923. Betty remembered attending a meeting of townspeople here in the grim, echoing gym before Christmas, not a true Town Meeting, just some concerned citizens sitting on uncomfortable folding chairs to discuss zoning issues. It hadn't meant much to Betty, who had only just moved to East Moulton, but Ted urged her to attend so she could meet her fellow residents. She hadn't gotten to know anyone then, but over the months, she'd managed to become acquainted with quite a few townspeople, mostly through her volunteer stint at the library—the regulars who borrowed books on Wednesdays when she was there, a few parents of the kids who had their Wednesday afternoon reading group, the kids themselves. As she was locking the car, she reminded herself to call and beg off volunteering at the library today and for the next couple of Wednesdays.

"Hi, Miss Trenka, going back to school?" Pretty, studious Denise Thomas, who took the library reading group very seriously, waved to her from the row of lockers at the end of the hall. One familiar face at least. Betty went to join her and two other girls. One of them was combing her red hair in front of a mirror on the locker door, while the other looked on critically.

"I'm going to be working here for a while, replacing

Mrs. Thurlow, who's out sick." The girls put on appropriately serious faces. "The thing is, I'm not sure where the principal's office is."

"Marcy knows," one of the girls teased, poking the perky red-haired girl with the comb. "She's spent half of her life sitting there waiting to be chewed out by Mrs. Carlson."

"That's not true!" Marcy said indignantly. "I help out in the office, and you know it. You're such a liar!"

"I'll show you," Denise said. "It's on the way to homeroom." The wide corridor with its vaulted ceiling was beginning to echo with young, very loud voices as the students assembled for the day. "The high school classes are mostly here in the old building, and the office is right down there," Denise said. "There was a big argument when the new building got built about whether the little kids should be there or here, so they decided that our classes would be here, the middle school is here, and the little kids have most of the new building. The high school has a few rooms there. Just for some classes, biology and art, but at least we get to look out the windows once in a while, even if all we can see is the playground and the woods out back." Denise walked along briskly, and Betty followed, conscious of the students' curiosity about the tall older lady with thick glasses in their midst.

"Here it is." Denise stopped in front of a wooden door with a window, through which some desks and rows of filing cabinets were visible. "There's the first bell. I've got to run. My homeroom teacher hates it when we're late. Hey, Kevin, wait up." Denise was gone, tagging after a tall, muscular boy who must surely be an athlete, but no one Betty recognized from the library or around town.

Betty opened the door and entered the room that was to be her new place in life. A door to another office was at the end of the room, but right before her was a neat desk with a computer terminal, a jar of pens and pencils, a container of paperclips, a telephone, all the usual familiar stuff of any business office. She felt immediately at home.

The other door had a plaque on it that read MRS. CARLSON. She knocked.

"Come in, how many times do I have to tell you not . . ."

Betty entered cautiously. "Mrs. Carlson? It's Elizabeth Trenka."

"I'm sorry if I sounded abrupt. Except for dire emergencies, the students aren't supposed to bother me in the morning. Am I glad to see you, Miss Trenka. Come on in and sit down. I'd offer you coffee, but that's one thing Ellen always used to do. I can't make coffee worth a damn." She covered her mouth with her hand. "I have to be careful to set a good example for the students, although I certainly wouldn't dream of using the language they do. The coffee thing is a long-standing office joke. I hope you know how to do it right."

"I believe I can," Betty said. "Although not necessarily as well as Mrs. Thurlow."

"First have a seat, and I'll explain what's expected of you. The usual paperwork; ordering supplies; some little correspondence for me; typing up messages to be sent home to parents; a daily bulletin that gets sent to all the teachers, reminding them of holidays, deadlines, things like that; anything else I want them to communicate to their classes or that I want to communicate to them. It's not easy having the whole range of ages in one school, but we're pushing to have a separate high school built up the road, where there's room for a sports field and a new science lab.

"East Moulton is growing pretty fast, lots of young couples moving in, and that means lots of new children to educate. I don't think it's such a good idea to have the little ones mixing in too much with the older kids." She frowned. "The older teens simply can't escape the impact of modern society, and that gets communicated to the little ones a bit too early for them to understand it all. Some of the high schoolers are pretty sophisticated characters." Then she smiled. "Sex, drugs, and rock 'n' roll, to put it concisely." Betty blinked and must have looked alarmed, because Sarah Carlson went on. "Now I don't want to give you the impression that this is a dangerous place. I've never seen any evidence of drugs, although sex in its more flirtatious forms is pretty rampant, as is rock and roll. All pretty ordinary stuff, and no big surprises for you."

"I don't expect I'll have much contact with the children, will I?" Betty asked.

"Only when they come dragging in here because they have to see me. Once in a very great while, some teacher will call in sick at the last minute before we can round up a substitute. Ellen used to take over the class, sit at the teacher's desk and look stern, give them an essay topic, even if it was a biology or physics class. She was always great at coming up with something they ended up enjoying. For the littler ones, she'd pick up a book in the library and have story hour, or have the middle schoolers tell about some adventure they've had."

"So I might have to do that," Betty said nervously. She wasn't exactly worried by the prospect, but she wasn't a particular fan of children of any age.

"Better you than me," Mrs. Carlson said. "In fact, just by virtue of not being me, you're assured of a warm reception. Don't worry, it doesn't happen very often, and you won't have any lunchroom duty. The teachers rotate being present in the cafeteria during lunch hour to keep some semblance of order. There's a teachers' lounge next door to this office so you can bring lunch from home and eat it in peace, or you can run over to Main Street and do errands or eat at the diner. The few remaining smokers tend to do that, since the school board decided to ban smoking in the teachers' lounge."

"I don't smoke," Betty said.

"That simplifies things," Mrs. Carlson said. "You'll also probably be asked to help some of the older kids fill out forms. College applications, scholarships, that sort of thing. We don't have a guidance counselor, although I'm trying to get that into the budget. Don't worry; the seniors have their college applications in, but there's always something they need help with. Ellen was generous with her time, giving advice and helping with little problems, and they may not remember that you're a different person, not necessarily willing to provide the same services."

"I'll do what I can," Betty said, and wondered just exactly what she could do. "I supervised quite a few young women at my last job, and many of them were just out of high school. I don't know if I could handle a third-grader."

"Third-graders don't have problems," Mrs. Carlson said, "or at least not the kind that entails more than a Band-Aid from the school nurse. No forms to fill out, no romantic tragedies to discuss. No cliques shutting them out, no locker break-ins. A simple, safe life. It's all pretty simple and safe here." Sarah Carlson stood up and escorted Betty to her desk.

"We have a private washroom over there where you can get water for the coffee. Now, we're going to be ordering textbooks for next year. Ellen left instructions, and after homeroom, one of the high school girls comes for the second period to help out. Marcy Evans is her name, and she knows the routine. So do the rest of them who help out. You won't have any problems after you get acclimated." She looked at her watch. "I have a meeting with a parent in half an hour. You can just buzz me on the intercom when he arrives. He'll probably be late. Ellen kept a calendar of my appointments there on the desk. Hold my calls if I'm with someone, no matter how hysterical the mother sounds. Soothe, and I'll get back to her. You have a nice day." Mrs. Carlson smiled and went back into her office.

Betty booted up her computer, then saw the coffeemaker on a table near the windows. Even if she wasn't dedicated to the domestic arts, she could make coffee.

It was all so peaceful and ordinary. She heard a bell ring for the start of the next class period. The sound of teenagers in large quantities rose briefly, then faded. She had a job.

The intercom on her desk buzzed, and Mrs. Carlson said, "Could you come in and get my notes for the daily bulletin? There are a few standard things we put in, so I'll show you copies of previous bulletins."

Betty went to the principal's office with a notebook and pencil, thinking that she'd never had a female boss in her life. In fact, she had more or less been the boss, because Sid Senior had left most of the administrative and personnel issues to her.

Betty returned with the material Mrs. Carlson wanted included in the bulletin, along with a handful of old bulletins with notes about what should be included in today's issue.

"Normally, I like to have this in the teachers' hands by the first period after homeroom," Mrs. Carlson had said. "I often have the things I want included by the afternoon of the previous day, but obviously, today is different. And Miss Trenka, when students are late, the high schoolers have to report to this office, and they'd better have a written excuse for tardiness, which we—I for now, and you when you get more familiar with the rules and routine—approve or disapprove. We sign a slip that gets handed to the teacher. The little kids don't go through that. They go straight to their classes, and the teacher keeps track of who's late. We run a weekly statistical thing on absentees and tardiness, and check on anyone who's been absent for more than two days in a row without us hearing why from a parent. Teachers turn in their absentee and late lists in the middle of the day, end of day for a few who are always behind. Chronic tardiness needs some action, although it's more often than not the fault of the parents. Well, it's a time-consuming job keeping track, but Ellen left detailed instructions for you. After my meeting with the parent, I'll be out to go over everything with you. Just get the bulletin done."

Betty nodded. Routine was soothing. She could do this job. Yesterday's optimism had subsided into a feeling of having a place. At last.

CHAPTER 7

THE COMPUTER and its programs were ones Betty was familiar with, so after she had reviewed Sarah Carlson's notes and previous bulletins, she quickly assembled a bulletin for the day. She noted with a bit of pride that Sarah Carlson had included the announcement that Miss Elizabeth Trenka would be the interim school secretary until Mrs. Thurlow recovered, and that all students were expected to assist her in any way possible until she learned the school routine. There was a reminder about the May Day dance on Saturday from seven to eleven o'clock, a note about Billy Gates's lost pencil case, and a stern warning that students who left school grounds at lunchtime were subject to disciplinary action. She brought the bulletin in to Sarah for her approval.

"Done already? It looks fine," Mrs. Carlson said. "You're a wonder. The bulletin will be on schedule after all. We'll need . . . twenty-two copies, I think. Ask Marcy, the girl who'll be here as soon as homeroom is over. She knows exactly how many are needed, and she'll carry them around to the classrooms. Is that parent here yet?"

"Not yet," Betty said.

"Like father, like son," Sarah said and shrugged wearily.

When Betty returned to her desk, a man was waiting. His hairline was receding, and faint wisps of light hair were carefully combed over to provide a poor illusion that there was more hair than there actually was. Fantasy/reality again. Still, he was not unattractive although his face looked a bit puffy and his expression was downright mean. He fidgeted as Betty took her seat, and he adjusted his tie nervously as though he wasn't sure why he was wearing it. With a sports jacket and trousers with a decent crease, he didn't look like a businessman, but rather like a middle-aged boy dressed up for an occasion.

Betty consulted the calendar on her desk. "Mr. Rockwell?" He nodded. "Just let me tell Mrs. Carlson that you're here. Have a seat." He sat, but continued to fiddle with tie, collar, and cuffs, scratch his ear, run his hand over the remnants of his hair.

Sarah Carlson swept into the room, greeted Mr. Rockwell graciously, and took him off to the privacy of her office.

Redheaded Marcy barged into the office and dumped a backpack on a chair. "Hiya again, sorry I'm late," she said. "I got cornered by this really, really boring girl. Are the bulletins ready for me to deliver? Mrs. Carlson said they'd probably be late 'cause it's your first day."

"It's just coming off the printer," Betty said. "You're going to have to help me a bit with the routine. Mrs. Carlson is busy, and I don't know . . ."

"Only thing that's regular is the daily bulletin," Marcy said cheerfully. "Once in a while there's a special bulletin. We don't have a loudspeaker system in this old dump, but they say if they build a new high school, we'll have everything we could want." She shrugged. "I'll probably be out of college before that happens. Sure, I'll be glad to help you, but I'm only here for this period. Once a week or so I'm here during study hall period in the afternoon. The other kids will tell you what we always do. Don't worry. But don't be surprised if people start showing up asking for advice. Mrs. Thurlow was really good about helping out, and she was pretty smart about everything, like boys and stuff. Oh, geez, Tommy. Are you late *again*?"

Betty looked up and saw that Marcy was addressing Tommy, her own personal lawn mower. He hung his head rather than respond to her. Betty thought he was blushing.

"Well, you better have a good excuse this time, 'cause Miss Trenka here is new at the job, and Mrs. Carlson told her everybody's got to have a written excuse." Marcy looked at Betty, as if to confirm what Mrs. Carlson probably said. Betty nodded.

"Good morning, Tommy." He mumbled something, but she noticed that he was gazing longingly at Marcy rather than addressing her. Aha! Marcy must be the girl he liked. Betty was proud of her deductive capabilities, or perhaps it was merely intuition based on blushes and attitude. Marcy, however, didn't seem greatly moved.

Marcy put out her hand. "Excuse, please." The boy took a crumpled slip of paper from his pocket and handed it to her but seemed to avoid touching her hand. She in turn handed it to Betty, who unfolded the note and read it. Tommy meanwhile took a seat by the door, as though this was a boring routine. Marcy said in a low voice, "It had better be an excuse from Mr. or Mrs. Rockwell." When

Betty looked confused, she added softly, "His mother or his father."

Betty was startled. "I didn't know Tommy's last name was Rockwell. I do know him, though. He's going to do some yard work for me. And I know his mother a little. Is there more than one Rockwell in the school?"

Marcy shrugged. "Not that I know of. Well, wait a minute. Mr. Rockwell and Tommy's mother were divorced last year, then he married this other lady with two little kids, so maybe they got his name now. They're in school here. You'd have to ask Mrs. Carlson."

Betty looked at the note. The handwriting was rather unpracticed although the spelling and grammar were adequate. *Please excuse Tommy for being late,* it said. *We had important business to attend to.* But the signature didn't look like Linda Rockwell or any kind of Rockwell. It was a scrawl, but it looked very much like *Bradley Melville*.

Marcy whispered, "If it's an okay note, you can send him to his class."

"And if it's not?"

"I guess he's got to see Mrs. Carlson."

"Mrs. Carlson is busy right now," she told Tommy, who was still sitting in the hard chair near the door. "You'll have to wait."

He looked up at her with a sullen expression. She took note of those empty eyes, now that he wasn't gazing at Marcy. Marcy, in any event, was still pointedly ignoring him as she counted out a pile of bulletins. "What's the matter? Mrs. Thurlow always takes my excuses," Tommy said. He sounded belligerent.

"I'm afraid I can't," Betty said kindly. "I'm not Mrs. Thurlow and I'm new here, you see, and I don't . . ."

"You just like throwing your weight around," Tommy said. "Think you're so powerful. Power is where it's at, and if I ain't got any, then you got it all. You and Mrs. Carlson and the teachers and the kids here. What do you say about that?"

Betty had never gotten into an argument with a fourteen-year-old, and she wasn't about to now. "That's enough," she said firmly. "Mrs. Carlson will be finished soon." Finished, apparently, with Tommy's own father. She tried to find a resemblance, but didn't see it. He was rather more like his mother or his cousins, the Whiteys.

Tommy's response was a burst of profanity, not especially harsh. Betty had heard far worse from the factory workers at Edwards & Son, but Marcy rolled her eyes and picked up the stack of bulletins.

"That's no way to talk to Miss Trenka," Marcy said. "Tommy Smart Mouth, that's what the kids call him," she said over her shoulder to Betty. The she walked out of the office while Tommy glared at her, but he refrained from answering her with more shock words. He just slumped in his chair, while Betty wondered if she should let Mrs. Carlson know he was here, given the fact that she was in conference with his father.

Betty sighed. When she worked for Sid Edwards Senior, and a similar situation arose, she'd have Sid's secretary let him know quietly that something was up that he ought to know about or she'd tell him herself. As the office administrator it was her job to save embarrassment and prevent untoward scenes. But she didn't know proper protocol here.

"I ain't waitin' around here," Tommy said. "If I can't go to my class, I'm leaving." He stood up. In spite of his attempt at bluster, Betty still thought he was an unprepossessing boy, not yet subject to the teenage spurts of growth that filled out the chest and stretched out height. Even his challenge to Betty was immature, as though he was almost certain he would be denied.

He was.

"Sit down immediately," Betty said calmly but firmly. He sat without protest but glared at her as though his look could nail her to the wall. She went to her desk, picked up the phone, and pushed the intercom button for Mrs. Carlson's office.

"I'm sorry to disturb you," Betty said softly, "but there's a situation you should be aware of."

Mrs. Carlson didn't dispute this, but simply said, "I'll be right out. Can you say anything?"

"Only Tommy Rockwell," Betty said.

"I see." She hung up and in a moment appeared at her office door. Mr. Rockwell was not with her.

"Ah, Tommy. Late again. Did you bring an excuse?" Mrs. Carlson sounded weary, as though she'd been through this many times before. Betty handed her the note from Brad Melville. "As usual," Sarah said. "All right. I'll sign a pass this time, and you can go to your class, but I want to see you here at lunchtime."

"Yes, Mrs. Carlson." Tommy was fittingly apologetic to the principal, but he cast one more hostile look at Betty.

Suddenly the office was invaded by a troop of healthy teenaged specimens. They're only boys, Betty told herself as the lead boy approached Sarah Carlson and towered over her. The other three surrounded Tommy and poked him in the chest playfully. Tommy cringed, then straightened up. What she heard was a chorus of "Tommy Smart

Mouth in trouble again?" Plus some profane teasing. For a minute Betty thought Tommy was going to cry, but he pulled himself up and departed, his excuse from the office clutched in his hand.

"Yeah, we're all late," the big boy said to Sarah. "I was driving the gang to school, and the car just stopped. Out of gas. I got Lou at the gas station to write a note when we pushed the car in for a fill-up." He shrugged. "It's the best we could do."

"I suppose it will have to do," Sarah said, and took the oil-spotted note. "Go along, and just leave Tommy alone, will you?"

"Principal's pet," the boy muttered.

"That Tommy. I don't know what we're to do with him," Sarah said when the office emptied. "And his father isn't much help. Claims people pick on Tommy, the teachers, the other students—well, you saw it happening just now. I understand Joe Rockwell's concern, but Joe thinks he's picked on too. He wants to see that something's done about his son, but you can't stop kids from teasing one another, try as you might."

"I see that Tommy doesn't go out of his way to make himself popular," Betty said. "Can't his father sit him down and give him a talking to?"

"Joe Rockwell shares custody of Tommy with his mother, so he has a right to be concerned, but he's not much help. He's got a huge chip on his own shoulder. I've spoken with the mother, and she sees the matter a little more dispassionately. Understands that Tommy is sometimes his own worst enemy. Very capable of inspiring the hostility in his classmates. I guess they sense vulnerability, the way animals sense your fear of them. Joe would be doing Tommy more good if he kept him away from this one." She waved Brad's "excuse." "I'm afraid Brad Melville encourages Tommy to act up." She sighed and returned to her office.

At the door, she stopped and said, "It doesn't help Tommy much that his mother is dating one of our teachers. The kids have picked up on that and there's a lot of teasing about it, which Tommy reacts to badly." She squared her shoulders and went into her office.

After a few minutes, Joe Rockwell stalked out of the office, his face red and his hands clenched in tight fists at his sides. Mrs. Carlson was behind him.

"No damned bitch like you is going to tell me how to raise my boy," he said angrily. "It's his mother who's turning him into a wimp. I take him fishing, hunting, things guys need to do. We go up to Boston for Red Sox games every summer, and he's over at my place practically every Sunday during the season to watch football. Even that's too much Tommy for my present wife. She's got her own kids to worry about. Linda just tells him to go read a book or play video games so she can spend Sunday afternoon fooling around with her boyfriend."

"Mr. Rockwell, we're not here to discuss child-raising methods or the emotional life of Tommy's mother, but to figure out why Tommy's grades have dropped so badly, and why he's always late for school."

"That's Linda's fault, not mine. I got my new family to worry about. She can't get up in time to get him breakfast and to school, 'cause she's been out to all hours with that guy of hers. And you know who I mean."

Mrs. Carlson looked at Betty from the corner of her eye,

and Betty promptly made herself scarce at the far side of the room, pretending to check something in the files.

"I think we should discuss these matters in my office at another time," Mrs. Carlson said. "I'm not sure that Brad Melville is a suitable companion for a boy of Tommy's age, and he certainly has no business writing excuses for Tommy's lateness. That's your job, or his mother's."

"Hey, Brad's okay," Joe Rockwell said. "And that Raven sure is something." He wore an almost salacious grin and looked as though he might go on about Raven, but wisely he merely said, "Brad brings a lot of kids together, so at least Tommy has some friends. Mikey Davis and Chad Havers. They're good kids. You know them."

"I do," Mrs. Carlson said. "But Mr. Rockwell, I repeat, it is simply not appropriate for Brad Melville to be writing excuses for Tommy's lateness, and in the future they will not be accepted. Could you come in on Thursday at the same time to finish our discussion?"

"I'm a working man," Rockwell said. "I don't have time to breathe, and I certainly don't have time to listen to your crap about 'lagging educational development' and 'emotional immaturity.' My boy is okay, you hear? I can't come in before next week. Tuesday."

He didn't wait to hear if that was okay with Sarah Carlson, but left the office without a backward look.

"Put him down for Tuesday at nine," Mrs. Carlson said. "He'll be here. He's not as bad as he sounded just now. And remind me to get in touch with Tommy's mother. I'd better see her as well. But on a different day. And thanks for alerting me about Tommy being here."

"I didn't think an excuse from Brad Melville was quite right," Betty said.

"You heard me. It isn't. Do you know him?"

"He does odd jobs for a neighbor, so I've met him and Raven. Frankly, Mrs. Carlson, I think Linda Rockwell is really trying to raise Tommy properly. Her sister is another neighbor of mine, and they're both nice women."

"I have no problem with Mrs. Rockwell," Sarah Carlson said. "I just see trouble coming, and I want to head it off. Has the bulletin been sent around?"

"Marcy took it a while ago," Betty said. "Is there something else I should be doing now?"

Sarah Carlson sighed. "I'm working on the budget for next year, so I'll want you to look up some figures from last year. Ellen has a disk with all the old budgets somewhere around her computer, and there should be hard copies in the files. I'll need last year's and the year before."

Betty was glad to have a task that wasn't emotionally charged. But she couldn't resist asking, "Should I not accept excuses from Brad Melville for tardiness? I mean, he doesn't have any standing. . . ."

"He does to the kids who hang out with him," Sarah Carlson said. "Unfortunately. I've asked around about him, even asked the resident state trooper if anything was known about him, but the police don't know anything negative . . . currently. I have heard he used to live here in East Moulton and was a genuine hellion back then, but he's not in trouble now, just works odd jobs around town, so there's nothing I can do. It's up to the parents to keep their kids away from him. I do what I can for the children, but I can't do everything."

CHAPTER 8

JUST BEFORE noon, Betty went to the teachers' lounge to eat a sandwich she'd brought with her.

"I'll stay here in the office through lunch," Sarah had told her, "in case Tommy Rockwell chooses to show up. He's not always good at following orders. You're free to get food in the school cafeteria or go anywhere you'd like. We don't allow the children to leave, except that seniors on the honor roll can go across the street to the pizza shop as long as they're back in time for class. I don't recommend the place for adults. It's . . . it's rather jarring on the nerves."

Betty thought she'd rather sit quietly and think about her first morning at work. She was also curious about the teacher Linda Rockwell was rumored to be dating, the man Linda had mentioned Tommy didn't get along with, who seemed to be a person Raven knew well. He might be in the lounge. She hadn't met any of the teachers yet, except for one young woman who'd dashed into the office to complain about a lack of crayons for her first-graders. All in all, it hadn't been a bad first morning.

She'd found the old budgets and summarized the details

to make the job of preparing a new budget easier for Mrs. Carlson. There hadn't been too much activity in the office otherwise. Marcy was replaced by another girl, Susan, at eleven, and since there was nothing much for her to do, Susan had spent her hour telling Betty about her difficult boyfriend and the "way cool" clothes on sale at one of the shops at the mall.

"Marcy said Tommy Rockwell was late again," Susan said. "What a dope. He really likes Marcy, but she can't stand him or his friend Brad. Marcy said that Brad tried to get her to join that group of his, and called her a flame-haired beauty and stuff. She thought he was coming on to her, so she won't even mention his name. But she did go to the movies once with Tommy, and when she turned him down for another date, he went like crazy and said he didn't have any reason to live. Isn't that the stupidest thing you've ever heard? I mean, like, he's just a kid like the rest of us. Like, I've cried over boys, but no boy has ever cried over me. And no boy ever said he couldn't live if I didn't go to the movies with him."

Susan would probably have gone on forever, but there were absentee lists for Betty to input into the computer, and there were two calls from angry parents who hadn't liked the idea of closing the school the day before. They'd been seriously inconvenienced having their children at home rather than at school. Betty's apologies didn't have much effect on their anger, and she could only promise that she'd have Mrs. Carlson return their calls. She had no idea if Sarah Carlson was conscientious about calling back, but it was the only way she could get rid of them.

Two children had been sent to the principal's office for

some infraction of school rules. One was a terrified little girl in tears who looked about as harmless as a kitten. Mrs. Carlson was kind as she explained slowly that it was wrong to keep talking in class when the other children were working, and didn't the others keep quiet when the teacher asked them to?

Little Mary returned to her class chastened.

"Chronic," Sarah Carlson said. "Can you imagine what she'll be like when she's grown up? She'll probably be one of those annoying people who talk out loud during movies or won't shut up while the others are concentrating on their bridge hands."

The other child sent for firmer counseling was Kevin, the strapping high school boy Denise had tagged after. He'd gotten into a fight with another boy over a difference of opinion on the virtues of some musical group.

"I don't think Marilyn Manson is worth fighting over, Kevin," Mrs. Carlson said. "People have different tastes. I think you just like fighting."

"Maybe," the boy mumbled. Then he looked the principal in the eye. "You got to stand up to people, show you've got power. Otherwise they'll walk all over you."

"Sounds like Tommy Rockwell," Betty said when he'd left with an hour-long after-school study hall as punishment. "He was also talking about power, and not having any. That boy looks pretty powerful to me."

"He is," Sarah said. "He tried to hit me once, but he was remarkably unprofane today. I hope you're not troubled by having curses rained down on you by babies."

"I'm not," Betty said. "Does it happen often?"

"Too often for my taste. I think parents don't take the

same responsibility today that our parents did, especially in your day."

So I'm a little old lady even to the principal, Betty thought. Mrs. Carlson was two, maybe three decades younger than Betty's sixty-four years. Her son Don was probably about fourteen, and likely in Tommy Rockwell's class.

"Are Donnie and Tommy in the same class?" she asked.

"Donnie's a year ahead. He skipped a grade," she added proudly. "They're not friends really, although I've reminded Donnie to be nice to Tommy because of his broken home. We don't have all that many divorces in East Moulton, so there's no subculture of single-parent children who can commiserate with each other." She added thoughtfully. "In fact, the few there are seem to gravitate toward Brad Melville. Unlikely as it may seem, they may see him as a substitute father figure. I have no proof or any reason to believe it's true, but I think of him as a pernicious influence. And those 'excuses' for Tommy! Ridiculous. He's written them three or four times. I guess I find his looks unnerving. He always seems to be sneering, and his eyes give me shivers."

Betty nodded her agreement. Brad's weird eyes seemed to stay with her. She could see them now staring out of his lean face.

"I've asked Tommy's mother if he would mow my lawn this summer," Betty said. "He's agreed to do it."

"I hope he will," Sarah said. "A little hard work and responsibility would be good for him."

"He was pretty annoyed when I wouldn't accept Brad's note," Betty said. "I may have lost my handyboy."

"You did the right thing," Sarah said. "It's the parents' job to offer excuses. Normally, I'd have both the parents in at the same time, but in the case of the Rockwells, there's still a lot of bad feeling because of the divorce. It would likely be counterproductive. Joe's got a wicked temper." Sarah went off to return calls and told Betty to enjoy her lunch as the lunch bell rang. Then Tommy appeared.

"I'll tell Mrs. Carlson that you're here," Betty said.

Tommy glowered. "Yeah, sure." He muttered something angry under his breath.

"You know, you'd have more peace of mind if you weren't always so angry," Betty said. "Life can be a lot of fun."

"How would you know, an old bag like you?"

"You'd be surprised what old people know," Betty said, refusing to be insulted. "We've had a long time to figure it out." She smiled kindly at him, and he almost managed a smile in return. "Go on in for your talk with Mrs. Carlson, and try to be a gentleman. You'd be surprised how much power that gives you." She thought she might have made a slight impression on him.

Now, as Betty reflected on her morning, she looked about the still-empty teachers' lounge. She could hear the kids outside the room on their way to lunch. There were a few overstuffed chairs, a long table with folding chairs, a pile of magazines and newspapers. Not especially comfortable or charming, but it was an escape from the shrill chatter of teens and preteens. She understood that there was another lounge in the new building for the elementary school teachers. Probably a lot more comfortable than this one, which wore the ground-in grime of three-quarters of a century.

In a few minutes, a stream of teachers flowed into the lounge, eyed her curiously, and mostly went about their business. A few bothered to introduce themselves.

"Hi, I'm Karen Brown, seventh-grade English," a tall and attractive young woman said. "You must be Ellen's replacement in the office. Betty Trenka."

"Elizabeth Trenka," Betty said, correcting her gently, although she was certain she'd be Betty to all and sundry as long as she worked here.

"Cindy, Larry, come meet Betty Trenka," Karen said, proving her right. "This is Cindy Harris. She teaches history in the high school, and Larry McGovern here teaches physics and is the football coach."

"Hi, Betty," Cindy said. "Don't let the kids get you down." She laughed. "That's my mantra. I share it with everyone."

"You got to see my prize lad today," Larry said. "Kevin, the one who got sent to the office for fighting with Newt Hastings. He's my fullback, and I like to see him keep up his aggressiveness in the off-season, but fighting over music in the hall is a lousy way to do it."

"I suppose it is," Betty said politely.

"Say, Betty. We're having the May Day dance on Saturday, junior high through high school. You wrote it up in the bulletin. Could you chaperon?" Cindy looked at Betty expectantly. "I really need another person. Larry and I can't do it alone, and everybody else claims to have prior engagements."

"Well, I . . . I've really never done anything like that," Betty said cautiously. "What does it entail?"

"Showing up and looking stern enough to keep the kids

from performing impolite acts on the dance floor, maybe encouraging the younger boys to ask wallflowers to dance. Oh yes, and keeping an eye out for kids who might be sneaking out to the parking lot. We've been lucky that drugs don't seem to be a problem around here, but romance is in the air, and, well, you know . . . There are usually a couple of heated arguments that could turn into fights. Don't worry, Larry will be there to nip those problems in the bud, won't you, Lar."

Larry winced. "As long as I don't have to wear a tux."

"That's just for the senior prom," Cindy said. "This one's pretty informal, nice dresses for the girls and jackets and ties for the boys. The prom doesn't happen until the second week of June. This is just a big party for everybody. The kids are having a great time thinking up decorations for the gym, although you'll soon see that the gym in this old building is gloomy enough to be Dracula's castle."

"I've seen it," Betty said. "I went to a citizens' meeting there last winter."

"I for one can't wait for the first selectman to announce that the town's going to build the new high school."

"Don't hold your breath," Larry said. "My sources at the Town Hall say it'll be put off for another three years at least. They're doing some kind of survey to figure out how many kids they'll have to accommodate, both in high school and the lower grades."

"They do that every year so Sarah can decide if any of us gets let go because there aren't enough students to teach, or more teachers should get hired because there are too many kids for the present staff to handle," Cindy said.

Betty shut out the sounds of discussion of school issues.

She wasn't going to be here long enough to form an opinion or express it.

As the lunch hour slipped away, several other teachers came by to introduce themselves, and she made a real effort to remember their names and subjects. So far, nobody had mentioned Linda Rockwell's beau. Then she heard someone say, "I think Tommy Rockwell should be in therapy."

She sat up and looked at the formidable gray-haired woman in a sensible suit who had spoken. It wasn't someone who had introduced herself to Betty. Cindy noticed Betty looking at the woman and said, "Miss Novak, I don't believe you've met Betty Trenka, Ellen's replacement. Betty, Miss Novak is our senior staff member."

"Been here for a good forty years," Miss Novak said. That made her close to Betty's age. "I'm teaching kids whose parents I taught. How do you do, Miss Trenka? I hope you'll find the school to your liking."

Betty smiled faintly. "It's been pleasant so far. Could I ask what you meant just now about Tommy?"

"He has certain problems," Miss Novak said. "I won't go into them here, but the teachers are aware of them."

"He's just a kid," Cindy said. "Sure, the other kids aren't crazy about him, and they pick on him, but he's bright. I have him in American history, and even if his grades don't show it, he's smart. I think his father is too harsh with him. Joe Rockwell looks like a mild-mannered milquetoast, but he's got a temper. I think that's why the mother left him, because he used to knock her around."

"Mrs. Harris," Miss Novak said sternly, "we do not gossip about the parents of our students." Cindy closed her mouth and looked ashamed.

"I apologize, Miss Novak," she finally said.

"But everybody says so," Karen Brown said. "I mean, stuff like that goes a long way toward explaining why a kid's the way he is. They say the father used to beat up on the kid as well. You never really know what's going on behind the scenes."

"We do *not* gossip," Miss Novak said. "I am going to the cafeteria to get some tea and soup. Does anyone care to join me?"

When no one answered, Miss Novak made a stately departure, leaving the room behind her in silence.

Betty said, "I suppose I could chaperon on Saturday, Cindy. I'm not sure how good at it I'll be."

"Great! It's not hard, and it's even kind of fun seeing the kids make a start at learning the social graces. And the juniors and seniors don't usually come, just late middle school and freshmen and sophomores. I'm still trying to talk my husband into coming, but he won't hear of it. I have a couple of other people I'm going to ask, and Sarah said she would drop in for a time." She grinned at Betty. "Nothing like the principal to keep order." She looked around the room. "Is Phil here?"

"Phil won't do it. He's scheduled for the senior prom, and he says he doesn't chaperon more than once a year," Larry said. "Besides, you know he's seeing Tommy Rockwell's mother. One of the kids said Tommy was going to ask Marcy, the cute little redhead in ninth grade, to the May Day dance. He's really got a crush on her. I don't think Mom's boyfriend and Tommy at the same dance would work. He needs to exercise his social skills without having someone keep an eye on him."

"Sounds like more gossip to me, Larry," Cindy said. "How do you know all this? Eavesdropping on the kids?"

"Naw. Donnie Carlson told me. He said Tommy told him that he'd asked that creep Brad Melville if it was okay to ask a girl out, and apparently Brad gave him a yes."

"Why does everyone seem to know Brad Melville?" Betty asked. "And need his approval for everything?"

The teachers looked at each other.

"He hangs around the school," Karen said. "With that girl Raven. At first we were worried it was some kind of sexual predator thing, but apparently it's not, at least not obviously. He gets the boys jobs doing work for people who need muscle, however underdeveloped. There's not a lot kids can do in East Moulton to make a little money, so Brad acts as a kind of employment agency."

"I've heard that," Betty said. "Miho Takahashi told me that Brad's boys are going to work on her farm this summer, harvesting the vegetables for her stand, and then help with picking apples in the fall."

"Must be in violation of some child labor laws," Larry said. "Still it's a good thing to keep them occupied."

"But I've always suspected that Brad takes a cut of their earnings," Karen said. "One of the kids hinted at it. It's sort of as if he's enslaved them, even if he does keep them busy."

"I've got a few who will have to do summer school unless they shape up in these last few months. That'll keep 'em busy," Larry said.

Betty felt entirely at ease now in these friendly, chatty surroundings. She was secretly eager to meet the Phil who was seeing Linda Rockwell and who maybe knew Raven.

East Moulton on the surface was certainly a quiet, orderly little town, and she felt that she had found her niche, but she couldn't help feeling that there was another, less pleasant reality beneath the surface.

CHAPTER 9

BETTY GOT to meet Linda's Phil in a somewhat unexpected way.

First, she looked at the personnel list after lunch and found only one Phil. Phil Rice taught math in the high school, but it appeared to be advanced calculus, so Tommy was probably too young to be in such a class. He was likely still struggling with simple algebra. At least he didn't have to sit at a desk under the watchful eye of his mother's boyfriend.

The encounter came after school was over at three. Sarah asked Betty to stand on the school steps as the children got onto the school buses.

"It keeps them a bit more orderly, having an adult watching," she said.

"No problem," Betty said. "I've just about finished everything in the office."

"We generally close the office at four," Sarah said, "although Ellen and I used to stay on if there was something that had to get done, and quite a few of the teachers stay later to work on the next day's lesson plans. I think Miss Novak sometimes stays until midnight. Well, she's a single lady, not many chores at home, and teaching is her life. Maybe if I'd had a Latin teacher like her, I'd still be spouting Virgil at appropriate moments."

"Does Tommy take Latin from her?" Betty asked.

"First year; he's only in ninth grade. Why do you ask?"

"I wondered if she had firsthand knowledge of him. She said she thought he ought to be in therapy."

"Most of us think that. He doesn't control his anger very well. Then sometimes he's so withdrawn that I wonder if he's suffering from some kind of depression. I'm not a child psychologist, but I'm going to suggest to his mother when she's here that he see somebody, get some help."

But then it was time to stand guard over the buses. There was some shoving and a lot of noise, but at last the buses moved off and Betty started to return to her office to shut down the computer and unplug the coffeemaker. At least Sarah had approved of her coffee-making skills, which pleased her inordinately. She felt she could try making coffee for Ted, once she fixed up the ramp so he could come to her house. She was fantasizing about amazing Ted with her simple skill when she spotted a familiar figure across the street near the pizza shop. The ubiquitous Raven, garbed in black as usual, was deep in conversation with a tall man who was definitely not Brad Melville.

I am too nosy for my own good, Betty told herself, and then decided that a ginger ale was what she needed to end her day. She headed across the street to the pizza shop.

"Well, if it isn't Miss Trenka," Raven said when she spotted her. "You seem to be everywhere I am."

"Or you are everywhere I am," Betty said. "I'm working at the school, as I think I mentioned."

"Then you must know Phil Rice." The man looked

Betty up and down. He was distinctly handsome, well built with wavy brown hair and nice, friendly eyes, quite different from poor Joe Rockwell. At least Linda knew how to pick an attractive beau.

"I'm afraid we haven't met yet," Betty said. "I just started today." She put out her hand. "Elizabeth Trenka, replacing Ellen Thurlow for a time."

"You were mentioned in the daily bulletin," he said. "I'm Phil Rice." He shook her hand firmly.

"Phil teaches all this weird math stuff," Raven said. "There's magic in numbers, you know." She looked at Phil with a sort of mild adoration Betty hadn't seen when Raven spoke to Brad. She looked, well, as innocent and vulnerable as a girl can, except this one had fingernails like talons and what appeared to be a silver skull on the chain around her neck.

"Numbers aren't magic, kiddo," Phil said. "At least not the way you define it."

"I just came across from school to get something cold to drink," Betty said. She was now putting together Raven's comment to Linda about being a man-stealer, and her reference to "our friend Phil." Linda apparently had some competition in the self-styled femme fatale. She opened the door to the pizza shop and was assaulted by a blast of rock music and voices. Plus the odor of garlic, spices, bubbling marinara sauce, and pizza. The place was packed with after-school munchers, but she saw a tall cooler at the back of the shop, with shelves loaded with soft drinks in cans and bottles. As she squeezed through the crowd, she saw Brad alone at a table with Tommy. Other boys hovered nearby, but they seemed to be keeping their distance. Brad was talking and Tommy was listening intently.

She'd had enough of Brad Melville and Tommy Rockwell for one day, but as she approached the cooler, Brad looked up at her and stared at her with those eyes from an ancient tomb. Tommy scowled. She was convinced her grass would never be mowed by him. She clearly hadn't established a bond of friendship, not after this morning.

"I hear you didn't like my excuse for Tommy," Brad said. He didn't sound angry, but he did sound arrogant, as though no one dared to deny Brad Melville's status.

"I'm new at the job," Betty said. "I don't know yet what is acceptable and what isn't." She turned toward the cooler.

"Just so you'll know in the future," Brad said, "what I say goes. Tommy and I went out early to look over a couple of things, and we didn't notice the time."

Betty didn't want to get into a discussion with the likes of Brad Melville about the time, what couple of things needed looking over or anything else, so she said nothing. Brad didn't like that either.

"Listen, lady. I want an apology, and so does Tommy."

"Young man, please don't address me that way. I take orders from my employer, not you. I don't make the rules."

"I break rules," Brad said. "And I make them. I make and break people too. Bet you won't forget that." He turned away from her, leaving her unnerved by the implied threat. She inched her way through the crowd toward the cooler. Over her shoulder, she saw Tommy again listening to Brad. She wondered if they were talking about her.

Betty plucked an icy can from the cooler and managed to get to the cash register to pay for it. Outside, Raven and

Phil were still chatting, but now Betty saw that he had an arm around her shoulders.

Oh dear, she thought, what if Brad comes out and finds them. I don't want to be a witness to unpleasantness. Or worse, Tommy could appear and see his mother's boyfriend in a slightly compromising pose.

But then she decided it was none of her business, and sometimes kids learn about life the hard way.

"I'll be seeing you," Betty said, and at the sound of her voice, Phil quickly removed his arm. "I noticed that Brad is inside with Tommy. . . ." Might as well warn them.

"Damn. He was supposed to meet me out here," Raven said. "And he's been in there all the time. Gotta go, Phil sweetie." She squeezed his arm affectionately and glided into the pizza shop.

Phil gazed after her, then turned toward Betty. "Ah, Miss Trenka, I suppose you're wondering what that was all about."

"Not at all," Betty said. "It is none of my business."

Phil was not to be deflected. "Raven's keen on all this magic stuff, and she thinks mathematics have some kind of special power."

"I'm hearing an awful lot about power lately," Betty said. "I don't know about numbers, except maybe on a profit and loss statement, where the figures do have a certain power, especially if they represent profit." But she couldn't help adding, "I also know that when you get beyond two in a relationship between men and women, there tend to be powerful forces at work, not always with a happy ending."

"Raven is nothing to me, Miss Trenka, just a friend. But

I'd appreciate it if you didn't gossip about this at the school. You see, I'm seeing someone else."

"Tommy Rockwell's mother, Linda," Betty said, then regretted mentioning it. It made her sound as nosy as Molly at the pharmacy. "Linda's sister is my neighbor, and Tommy is going to do some chores for me. I'm not really a gossip."

"I hope he measures up as a worker, but he's got a few problems," Phil said. "He doesn't like me much. At least I don't knock him or his mother around. They're well rid of Joe, if you ask me."

"I'll be seeing you around school," Betty said, effectively putting a stop to further discussion about the Rockwells. She wasn't comfortable hearing about personal secrets. Then she felt she had to say, "Do you think it's good for Tommy to be spending so much time with Brad Melville and Raven?"

Since Raven was Phil's old friend, maybe she had offered some believable reason for the couple's appeal to kids.

"Raven's okay. I'm trying to convince her to dump Brad, because he's scum," Phil said. "I don't know what hold he has over them, over Raven. Linda says she doesn't like him, but he hangs around her place a lot. I'm afraid she's falling under his spell too. I guess it's like a cult or something, where the leader has the power to enchant his followers. Hmm, there's power again. That guy's got it, but he's a little crazy, if you ask me. Linda had him to dinner once when I was there, so I've heard some of his stories. He put on quite a performance to impress me, maybe Linda as well. He makes himself sound like Zorro and Superman rolled into one. The boys probably believe every word; you know kids."

Betty, of course, didn't, but she let it pass. "I've tried to persuade Tommy not to see so much of him," Phil said. "Just short of forbidding him to, not that he'd pay any attention to that. It's probably why he doesn't like me. I'd spend more time with the boy, but Joe doesn't like that one bit. He's flown off the handle a couple of times when he thought I was trying to take his place with Tommy. I'm not. I like Linda, enjoy her company, but I'm not planning on getting married any time soon. I had one bad marriage that ended a few years ago. Linda and I have a good time together, and that's enough for me."

Betty didn't know what to say. The more she tried to avoid hearing about other people's lives, the more she seemed to hear. Poor Tommy must be deeply confused by all this adult behavior. It was a far cry from asking a girl to the movies.

"I'm to be a chaperon at the spring dance," she said by way of changing the subject. "Someone said you'd refused to do it."

"I'm doing the senior prom. Linda said that Tommy wants to ask some girl to the May Day dance, and he wouldn't want me around while they were snuggling on the dance floor. He likes this girl named Marcy, a ninth grader, but she's stuck on one of the boys in my calculus class, although she did go to the movies once with Tommy. His first real date. Now Linda says he's getting up courage to ask her to the dance and is scared to death she'll turn him down. I don't remember things being so serious when I was a kid."

"I wouldn't want to be young again," Betty said. She

did remember how serious the social scene had seemed when she was young, and still had vivid memories of not being asked to her school dance. "I'm not even sure that I'm up to being a chaperon in the fullness of my years."

"Chaperoning's not so bad," Phil said. "Larry McGovern's going to be there, and he asks all the ladies to dance. You'll have a good time. The kids generally behave themselves."

Betty wasn't much of a dancer, and she hoped that Larry would understand if she turned him down or worse, stepped on his toes.

"I've got a few things to finish up in the office," she said. "I'll probably see you tomorrow." And she finally escaped from Phil and his romantic problems. She would make an effort to avoid further confidences and tangled relationships.

Her ginger ale was warmish, but she drank it anyway as she put away the things on her desk. Sarah locked the door to her office and gave Betty the keys for both doors.

"Here are the items for tomorrow morning's bulletin. I'm going home to try to get all those numbers out of my head for a few hours. See you in the morning," Sarah said. "Miss Trenka, you're going to work out just fine. I'm so glad we found you."

"And I'm glad I found you," Betty said. She decided she'd stay here a while and draft tomorrow's bulletin, which she'd finish up in the morning. Then she was looking forward to Penny Saks's spaghetti dinner. She found herself especially looking forward to tomorrow. Only for a moment was she troubled by her encounter with Brad. She remembered that his tight T-shirt showed a powerful chest and well-defined biceps. He would not dare harm her, would he?

Dinner at the Sakses' was anything but quiet, but it certainly was good, and Betty put from her mind the unsettling effect Brad had on her at the pizza shop. She forgot the hypothetical Phil/Raven/Linda triangle. She didn't even care if her flowers were blooming.

"I saw you at school today," one of the Whiteys said.

"I'm working in the office for a while," Betty said. "You see that you behave so you don't get sent to see the principal."

"I don't do bad stuff," Whitey said. "And Mrs. Carlson's okay, unless you're really bad. Tommy's always getting sent to see her. One time he threw a chair at his teacher. Boy, did he catch it that time."

"That'll be enough, Ned," Greg Saks said. Betty was surprised that the Whiteys actually had other names, but of course they would. She'd just never heard what they were, and wondered what the names of the other two really were.

"But he did! All the kids know about it." He looked to his brothers for confirmation, but they were busy finishing their plates of spaghetti. Ned wrinkled his nose and stuck out his bottom lip. "He didn't get the teacher, though," he said under his breath.

"You heard your father," Penny said. "You and Will go get the ice cream from the freezer. Patrick can bring the cookies." At last, all of the Whiteys had names, even though she was sure she wouldn't remember which was which. They almost looked like triplets.

"Poor Linda," Penny said to Betty later, as they loaded

the dishwasher. "Tommy's always in trouble. I think he learned about letting off anger in inappropriate ways from Joe, so he's probably better off now that Joe's not around all the time. Still . . ."

"I met Joe today," Betty said. "He was in to see Mrs. Carlson. Then I met Linda's boyfriend. Phil Rice. He seems nice enough."

"Linda thinks the world of him. I can tell by the way she talks about him, although she hasn't said much about any plans for the future. I hear he's got a bit of a reputation as a ladies' man," Penny said, "but he is good-looking. I met him at a parent-teacher night. I'll say this. He and Joe definitely don't get along, not that they meet very often."

Betty said carefully, "I had the impression that he's not looking to settle down." Not if he has Raven clinging to him.

"Then I don't know if he's good for Linda in the state she's in," Penny said. "She'd like to find a new husband, and have more kids."

Betty felt she had said enough and didn't mention seeing Phil with Raven. Ladies' man, indeed. Well, he did have the looks. All the teenaged girls at the school were probably studying hard in their math classes to be eligible for calculus with Mr. Rice.

Betty was pleasantly tired when she finally got to bed around ten. Even Tina appeared to have mellowed out, after a day home alone without Betty to harass with pleas for food. The bowl of dry cat food was empty, so she'd been given a hefty spoonful of tuna to let her know she hadn't been completely abandoned. Betty nodded off, with the faint odor of tuna breath floating up from the foot of the bed.

Life seemed very good, until the phone woke her near midnight.

It was Miho, who sounded so upset that Betty had difficulty understanding her.

"It was terrible," Miho said. "Thieves in the night, smash, crash."

"Calm down," Betty said. "Tell me slowly what happened."

What had happened was that Judit's RV had been broken into, and Judit herself had been knocked unconscious by the intruder. Miho had put her nursing skills to work and had looked after her, but had finally arranged to send her by ambulance to the hospital in the neighboring city. The police had been summoned, but they said it wasn't possible to tell how much had been stolen, except that Miho saw at once that Judit's prized gold necklaces, earrings, and other jewelry were gone. They'd found some bullets in a drawer, but no gun to go with them, so they were going to have to ask Judit if she had owned a gun that had been stolen.

"Are you all right, Miho? Do you want me to come and stay with you?" Betty asked, when Miho had come to the end of her breathless account. "Or you can come here; there's a spare room if you don't want to stay there alone."

"It's okay," Miho said. "I should not have wakened you, but when the ambulance was taking her away, Judit asked me to tell you. She kept saying that she had told you it was an evil day, and you would understand."

"Maybe I do," Betty said. She wondered if Judit was trying to tell Betty that the evil day that she believed was related to Brad and Raven meant that they had been involved in the attack. "Are you sure you don't want to leave your house? They could come back."

"Do not worry," Miho said. "I will be all right. I have a gun myself. My husband gave it to me. He always liked weapons, and he taught me to shoot straight. If anyone comes back to break into my house, I will not allow them to do so."

Too much waving of guns around to suit Betty, but she was reassured about Miho's immediate safety, unless someone planned to steal one of her expensive orchids. Hadn't Miho mentioned that Raven craved an orchid?

"In the morning, Miho, check to see that your orchids are all there. If any are missing, please tell me."

Miho was silent for a moment, then said, "I understand. You are too kind to accuse someone without proof. I will look now, to be sure the greenhouse door is locked and my babies are safe. I will telephone you in the morning if all is not well."

as about ... something ... well, she hadn't quite gotten it.
[indistinct faded text at top]

CHAPTER 10

THE NEXT morning, Betty was as eager to get to work as she had been on her first day. The weather continued to be beautiful, and a quick inspection of her flower patch showed that nothing had keeled over in the night.

However, this day was slightly blighted by her concern about poor Judit, lying in a hospital with unknown injuries. She decided she would drive to the hospital after work to see her. And she would await Miho's promised call to hear anything further about the circumstances of the break-in.

Today she arrived even earlier than the day before, because she wanted to polish the draft of the bulletin before Sarah Carlson arrived. It would be ready for distribution before the first classes began. She was also wondering if Tommy had gotten up the courage to invite Marcy to the May Day dance, which was only two days away, but she wasn't sure if that was a question she could ask openly. If Marcy had been asked and had turned him down, she wasn't likely to admit it to the school secretary. She didn't know a lot about young people, but she did know from her days at Edwards & Son that girls didn't mind sharing news of happy moments, but were less forthcoming about painful ones.

Since she was so early, there weren't many kids hanging around the parking lot, and the school buses hadn't arrived yet, but a few teachers' cars were parked in the lot. She spotted Miss Novak making her stately way up the steps and into the building.

Betty herself had studied Latin for a couple of years in high school, much to her father's disgust, since he didn't feel a future housewife needed what he called "lessons in nonsense." Poor Pop never did see his dreams of a husband and family for Betty come true. He was more eager for that than even her mother, who had once remarked that being a housewife with a demanding spouse wasn't all it was cracked up to be. Not that Pop was a bad guy at all, but he could be demanding, and Ma put up with him with more cheerfulness than Betty would have.

Betty loved studying Latin, and her teacher made Roman history come alive as they pored over the pages of text. Of course, in those long-ago days, Latin was an element of life because the Mass was still conducted in Latin, and Betty always thought that if she knew the language, she could talk with anyone in the world who went to a Catholic church. She was disappointed to discover that wasn't true, but in any case, she never got beyond Caesar and the Gallic Wars.

Pop had demanded that she drop Latin after the second year and take home economics, in which she didn't do as well as in Latin class. Her lack of competency in the domestic arts was something that went way back to girlhood. The only thing besides coffee that she made reasonably well was her mother's bean soup with dropped noodles, a recipe that Ma had inherited from Betty's Czech grandmother.

The long dark hallway of the school was remarkably silent this morning. She entered the darkened office and felt the familiar pleasure of turning on the lights to bring the place to life. It was a simple act that reminded her vividly of the old days at Edwards & Son, where she was always the first to arrive. The offices were always warm and silent, and she could still hear in her mind the distant sounds of the factory in the big building behind the offices. The early factory shift started much earlier than even Betty, who would check Sid's desk to be sure he had a yellow lined tablet and a jar full of sharpened pencils to get him through the day. That should have been his secretary's responsibility, but she was young and comparatively careless about details, far too wrapped up in her boyfriend, who was one of Edwards & Son's junior salesmen. Those days were gone forever, and it was pointless to hark back to them. In fact, Betty told herself sternly that it was time to stop harking back to the past. She had a new life now, and what was over was over.

After booting up the computer, Betty put the finishing touches on the bulletin and printed off the right number of copies. Then she made coffee so it was ready by the time Sarah arrived. Sarah approved the bulletin and went to her office with coffee cup in hand to face the budget chore.

Eventually Betty heard the voices of arriving students outside in the hall, and just before time for the bell to announce the first class, the telephone on her desk rang.

"Is that Miss Trenka?" The woman's voice was familiar. "It's Linda Rockwell," the caller said. "I . . . I wanted you to know that Tommy won't be in school today."

"Is he ill?" Betty asked.

"No," Linda said shortly. "He'll be there tomorrow. We had a little problem at home last night." Then she hung up abruptly.

Betty frowned. Linda had been much friendlier at the dress shop. She'd sounded downright angry on the phone. Thinking of the dress shop reminded Betty that she literally didn't have a thing to wear to a school dance. Surely the chaperons were expected to look nice, to set a good example for the kids. She didn't think she'd need a formal gown, but certainly something more festive than what she owned. As she made a note to indicate that Tommy's mother had called in an excuse for his absence, she started wondering what Tommy had been up to. Linda's voice had been tight with what? Annoyance? Anger?

Peaceful East Moulton obviously had a lot of things going on under the surface that weren't entirely pleasant, but at least she wouldn't have to deal with a late-for-school excuse for Tommy from Brad Melville.

Marcy showed up to get the bulletins, and Betty noticed that she was subdued. She didn't smile once, and her usual cheerfulness wasn't there. Her eyes were red as if she had been crying.

"How are you today?" Betty asked kindly, trying not to show that she'd noticed Marcy's mood.

"Lousy," Marcy said. She bit her lip as though to keep control of her emotions. "Life is lousy. Why can't everything be nice?"

"I wish I could answer that," Betty said. "Do you want to tell me about it?"

Marcy shook her head, but started to tell her anyhow. "It's nothing. People are just stupid, especially boys. They always think you should go along with what they want, like you don't have a mind of your own. I mean, like, no means no, right? And you don't have to explain why you don't want to do something, and you don't have to put up with threats if you say no. I mean, nobody owns me." Marcy turned indignant.

Betty took this to mean that Tommy had asked her to the dance, and she hadn't wanted to accept. Well, she certainly had the right to refuse, but from her words, Tommy hadn't taken the rejection well, not if his response had been threats. Perhaps he felt bad enough to stay out of school for a day. Maybe it would make Marcy feel better if she knew she wouldn't have to face him today.

"We won't have to worry about Tommy Rockwell being late today," Betty said. "You won't have to worry about seeing him at all. His mother called to say he wasn't coming to school today."

"Good," Marcy said. "I don't want to see his face after what he said to me." Betty waited, for she was sure Marcy would tell her more, and she did.

"Tommy asked me to the May Day dance last night, but I'm hoping someone else, someone I really like, will ask me, even though it's getting pretty late, so I said no to Tommy. Then he said I'd ruined his life, and he wished we were both dead and a lot of other stuff. Hey, there are a lot of girls in the school who would probably go with him. Why does he keep picking on me?"

"Marcy dear, you should be flattered that someone feels so strongly about you, and then just forget the bad parts.

Maybe the boy you want to go with will ask you after all, and pretty soon you won't even remember this."

"Tommy will," Marcy said sulkily. "He said he'd never forget how much I hurt him. He said I'd tell everybody and they'd tease him more than they do now. I swore I wouldn't mention it, but he wouldn't believe me. Said he had ways of shutting me up. He scared me. I'm afraid he'll tell Brad and he'll do something to me."

Betty wasn't convinced that teenaged crushes were quite so enduring and dramatic. She couldn't even remember the name of the first boy she'd fallen for, but he'd gone off to fight in World War Two and had died young. She'd cried for him, she remembered that, but now he was just a dim memory. After him, the only man in her life had been Sid Edwards Senior, and he remained so to this day. Her mind wandered away from Marcy's problems and went to Sid. She'd visit him on Sunday, after she'd supervised her Saturday lawn mowing and chaperoned at the dance. She'd have some tales to tell him as he lay there in his nursing home bed without speech and movement.

Except for the unhappy Marcy, the school day moved along without incident, and Betty felt even more at home today. The tasks were routine rather than stimulating, but she supposed that at her age, she'd had enough stimulation in her life. Concern about Judit's state troubled her some, but a phone call to the hospital told her that the old lady was resting comfortably.

Then Miho called to tell her that someone had tried to get past the lock on the greenhouse door, but had failed. Her orchids were safe. She had spoken with the doctor and had assured that Judit was not seriously damaged.

"She will be allowed to come home tomorrow, Friday," Miho told Betty. "It is good that she has Medicare to pay. One would not have thought that she would think to arrange that, since she seems so foreign."

"I plan to visit her after work," Betty said, "so she won't feel alone, and I can bring her home from the hospital tomorrow. Have the police said anything more about the break-in?"

"The state trooper was here today to look again at the RV, and he brought some men to look for fingerprints, I suppose. He said that he believes it was bad boys who wanted to steal her gold jewelry."

"Miho," Betty said slowly, "I've been wondering. Could it have been her grandsons? They knew she had the jewelry, and maybe even money in the RV. If she owned a gun, they would have known that, too. They certainly are bad boys, as I know from experience, and she surely would have recognized them, but she would never tell the police about them. I'll ask her when I visit her this afternoon. Maybe she'd tell me." Judit would also have recognized Brad and Raven, but she didn't want to mention them to Miho, lest she be frightened that they would come back. Raven seemed to be the only person who would be tempted to steal a delicate, expensive orchid.

"Unless those boys walked here, I would have heard their old truck drive up," Miho said. "I was up until late watching television. Because she hadn't felt well for these past few days, I decided to see how she was before I went to bed. That's when I found her lying on the ground unconscious, with a cut on her head. Everything in the RV was thrown about even worse than it usually is. I just don't know who could have done it. But maybe you can persuade her to stay in the house with me when she leaves the hospital."

"Or with me," Betty said. "I certainly have room for her." Only weeks before, Judit had tried to convince Betty to let her live in the house on Timberhill Road, to cook and clean and be her friend, and now it might come to pass. Betty didn't relish a roommate but what could she do? Old ladies have to help each other.

At lunchtime, Betty found Phil waiting for her outside the teachers' lounge.

"I need to talk to you," he said. "Let me drive you to Main Street and we can grab a bite at the diner."

Betty was puzzled. She could think of no reason that Phil needed to say anything to her, unless he wanted to persuade her to take his side in his quest for some new and very expensive textbooks. She'd noticed his requisition among the many others she was processing for next year.

"It would be a nice change from my tired old sandwich," she said, and walked out to the parking lot with him. Phil's taste in cars seemed to be as expensive as his taste in calculus textbooks. He drove a shiny black Mercedes with red leather seats and a lot of fancy dials on the dashboard. It made her sedate Buick look almost prehistoric.

Phil drove her into town in a style to which she had never been accustomed, and escorted her into Matthew's Diner and Café, where she'd once stopped on a cold day last winter for a bowl of soup. It had booths and a long counter with stools occupied by businessmen and laborers seeking a cheap lunch. The requisite perky blond waitress dashed efficiently from booth to booth taking orders and delivering plates of food. Betty noticed a couple of teachers from the school in one booth, apparently grading papers while they ate their lunch.

"It's not too glamorous," Phil said, "but people tend to leave you alone." He steered her toward the last booth, away from the other teachers.

"I'm not much of a glamour person," Betty said, "but I do like to have my lunch in peace." She glanced at the menu. Meatloaf with a side of macaroni and cheese was the special of the day. It sounded like true comfort food to her, and when the waitress appeared at the table, that's what she ordered.

"Matthew's got that lentil soup you like so much today, Phil," the waitress said. She was flirting with him, which only reinforced his reputation as a ladies' man.

"Okay, hon," Phil said.

"What's up?" Betty asked as the waitress departed. She couldn't imagine why Phil Rice needed to speak with her in private. Surely he knew that as a temp, she had no influence over textbook purchases.

"Two things, maybe three." He hesitated. "One, I wanted to be sure you didn't get the wrong idea about me and Raven. She's sort of a pal; I've known her for years. I met her when she was a senior in high school in a little town near the Rhode Island border. I was teaching freshman algebra, and she was on the way to perfecting her femme fatale look. I noticed her, but I never dated her—I'm careful about that student-teacher thing—but as I say, it was a small town, smaller than East Moulton, so I got to know her. Imagine my surprise to find that she was now living here. I guess she's always kind of had a crush on me. It makes her sort of possessive, since we go back such a long time. I mean, she's said some pretty bad things about Linda, but I don't think Linda knows anything about my long acquaintance with Raven. Unless she heard it from Brad."

"I don't think I have any ideas about you two, and certainly not a wrong one," Betty said. "I know you've been seeing Tommy Rockwell's mother, but I scarcely know her, so I certainly wouldn't have occasion to mention seeing you with Raven."

Phil relaxed a bit at that, then said, "Second thing. It's mostly Tommy I wanted to talk to you about. You said he works for you."

"Will work for me. Mowing my lawn and a few little chores. He hasn't started yet, and I really don't know him either. He's not very happy with me in any case, since I gave him a hard time about an excuse for being late written by Brad Melville."

"Do you know Brad Melville well?"

"Only in passing," Betty said. "He does some chores for my neighbor."

"As I said, I'm trying to wean Tommy away from him. He's a bad influence. But Linda seems to think it's good for Tommy to have an older guy to pal around with. Tommy doesn't like me because I've told him no once too often. I think it makes him all the more eager to spend time with Brad. Then I'm afraid Linda's getting mixed up with him."

"Brad and Linda?" Betty thought that close to impossible, but maybe they felt like ganging up against Phil and Raven. "Why do you think Brad is such a bad influence?" She couldn't help thinking it herself, but she wanted to know Phil's reasons. "And why would Linda want to involve herself with him, of all people?"

Phil looked uncomfortable. "I believe he's as violent as Joe, so maybe she's used to that. Sometimes dangerous men are attractive to women. I don't know. Raven has told me that he thinks nothing of hitting her. . . ."

Betty winced. She was hearing about entirely too much domestic violence for a town like East Moulton. But then, she herself had witnessed Raven goading Brad into striking her.

"Another thing about Brad," Phil said slowly. "There have been some robberies around town. Raven says I'm just trying to pin something on him, but we never had such a thing before he got here. He doesn't work, except for his odd jobs, but he always seems to have plenty of money. And nobody likes the way he controls the boys who think he's such hot stuff. Who knows what he'll put them up to?"

"Is it true that he takes a cut of whatever they earn through jobs he's set up for them?" Betty wondered if anyone would ever corroborate that story.

"I wouldn't doubt it, and the kids would never tell on him."

"Are they that loyal, or does he have some kind of power over them?"

"Only the power of an intriguing personality and history, as far as I know," Phil said. "And don't start thinking drugs. People have been checking on him, just because he is so popular with the kids. Nothing suspicious there, and no sign that drugs are around the town or the school. If he has criminal tendencies, selling drugs to schoolkids isn't among them. I guess that makes East Moulton a rarity, in this day and age."

"Did you hear about the robbery last night?" Betty asked. "The old woman who lives on Miho Takahashi's property was knocked around a bit and is in the hospital. Some things were stolen."

The waitress appeared with their food, and Phil crumbled crackers into his soup, waiting for her to leave before he answered Betty.

"I did hear something. In small towns like this one, you hear things almost as soon as they happen. Linda had gotten a call from that awful woman at the drugstore, what's her name? Molly, who seems to know everything. She'd seen Tommy riding his bike through town quite late at night last night, and hoped he was okay because there were dangerous people abroad beating up old ladies. Then she told Linda the whole story. Tommy wasn't home yet, so Linda called me, totally frantic about what to do. It turned out that Tommy had gotten up courage to ride over to Marcy's house to ask her to the dance."

"And he was turned down," Betty said. "I heard about it from Marcy. Poor kid. So he just kept riding, I suppose, until the hurt went away. Diminished. He'll get over it."

"It's bad for the kid's ego," Phil said. "Anyhow, he finally got home while Linda was still talking to me so no harm done."

"Except that he didn't come to school today."

Phil ate his soup in silence for a while, then said, "I wonder if our friend Brad Melville could have had anything to do with robbing the old lady. I wouldn't think he'd know her."

"He does," Betty said. "He and Raven have visited her

because Raven thinks old Judit knows about magic, and Raven seems to think she'd like to be a witch."

Phil smiled. "She's talked about that since she was in high school. I've told her there's no magic in this little corner of Connecticut, just like there wasn't any near the Rhode Island state line, but she's still into some pretty weird stuff. Right now she's talking about Beltane, May Day, which is supposed to be an important holiday for witches. She's got a pile of books about it all."

"I understand she reads a lot," Betty said. "Well, Judit told her to forget about magic, too, but still, the two of them do know Judit; they've been to her place, they've seen her jewelry that she's never without, which was stolen. If any of those gold chains shows up on Raven's lovely neck . . ."

"I wouldn't put anything past Brad, but Raven's okay, just a little confused by all this New Age stuff. I think she believes that if she can cast spells, she'll have power over everything, and be rich. Power, power. It's gotten to be like a refrain. Tommy wants the power to make Marcy like him and go to the dance with him. Brad enjoys his power over the kids. Joe Rockwell still wants to retain his power over Linda, even though he left her."

"And what kind of power do you want?" Betty asked.

Phil shrugged. "Not much. Maybe the power to cram some knowledge into a couple of my students' heads." Then he smiled. "But that power is in me, if only I use it right. How about you?"

Betty thought for a minute. "I'd like the power to turn back the clock a couple of decades, to be back where I was twenty years ago." A picture of Edwards & Son's offices flashed briefly through her mind, but she had told herself to stop looking back. "But that's not possible, so maybe I'd settle for the power to make the flowers I've just planted grow tall and healthy."

"I think you probably have that in you," Phil said. "All it takes is patience and a watering can."

They were a little late getting back to school, but neither of them had specific duties in the ten minutes they weren't there. Betty apologized to Sarah Carlson for being late, but Sarah just dismissed the issue with a wave of her hand and returned to her budget.

Betty didn't see Marcy for the rest of the day, and before she knew it, the day was done. After she'd seen the school buses depart, Betty got into the Buick and headed for the hospital where she hoped to find Judit alert and willing to talk to her, since she had probably evaded all questions from the police.

Judit, Betty suspected, was wary of officialdom, possibly for very good reasons.

CHAPTER 11

JUDIT WAS in a small ward with seven other old women, the beds divided from one another by white curtains. Some of the old ladies moaned quietly, but none of them seemed to have elaborate medical equipment attached to them, so they couldn't be terribly ill. One or two of them had visitors, grown children or friends, and all of them seemed to have large floral bouquets on the tables beside their beds. Betty felt momentarily guilty that she hadn't brought flowers for Judit.

Judit was dozing, but her eyes flew open as soon as Betty pulled the curtain aside and stood beside the bed.

"How are you feeling?" Betty realized that this hospital stay might help with the pain Judit had complained about. If something was wrong with her, the doctors should find it.

Judit put her hand to her forehead, which had a large bandage on it right up to her red hair. It was time for more henna, because gray roots were beginning to show.

"I am alive," Judit said weakly. "But no thanks to those cowards who beat me."

"Cowards? There were more than one?"

"I don't remember," Judit said. "But they took my gold, the things that my husband gave me. He was such a good

115

man, a good husband, you should have had such a man." A tear appeared at the corner of her eye. "I will never get them back, I know it, and it will be no good to replace them. He gave them to me back in the old country when we were young, before my sons were born. He was such a good man."

"Do you know who robbed you?"

"The policeman in a uniform like the Nazis who crushed our people, he asked me that, but I tell him nothing. I do not know who creeps up to my RV in the night and tears the necklaces from my throat. I was sitting outside beside the fire, and suddenly they were there. But it was too dark to see them."

"So there *was* more than one."

Judit raised her head from the pillow and seemed to nod.

"But you had the fire, so it wasn't completely dark."

"It was dark," she said. "It was only a little fire. Miho doesn't like a big fire near the house."

"Isn't there anything you can tell me? They weren't your boys, were they?"

"No! My grandsons would not dare to do such a thing to me. I cooked for them and washed their clothes. They would not dare. They know I would put a curse on them, the most terrible curse they could imagine. Worse than they could imagine. Their skin would itch with red scabs, women would no longer look at them, their stomachs would not hold food, and they would lie on the ground screaming in pain." She looked at Betty with something like satisfaction. "That is what I would do." Maybe Judit did have a couple of magic spells up the sleeve of her denim shirt. She certainly sounded convincing.

"You must have seen something that could identify

them." Betty was certain she knew something, because Judit made a big show of closing her eyes and sighing deeply.

"Now, Judit, you can trust me. Please tell me, or the police."

The eyes fluttered open. "I do not speak to the police," Judit said. Then she relented. "But you are my friend, Elizabeth, so I will tell you that they came like shadows, all in black. Except that I saw a flash of silver when they attacked me and tore away my gold chains, and my bracelets and the earrings my husband gave me when our first son was born."

"Did you own a gun?" Betty asked, fairly certain that Judit would not be truthful, but she was thinking of Raven's silver skull on a chain glinting in the faint light from the fire.

"It was just a little one," she said. "The boys gave it to me so I would feel safe when I was alone, but I have never used it. I keep it in the little wooden chest in the RV. And the bullets somewhere else."

"Then the gun was stolen too," Betty said. "The police said they have found bullets, but no gun. This could be serious, if it was kids who took it."

"They were not children," Judit said firmly. "Tall, well-grown people. A man and a woman. I could smell her perfume."

"Could it have been . . ." Betty hesitated. "Could it have been Brad and Raven?"

Judit closed her eyes again. "An evil day. Whoever commits evil loses power." She smiled to herself. "That will spoil her dreams."

"So it was Raven. And Brad."

"I did not say so."

"I think the police should be informed."

"Don't trouble them," Judit said. "Punishment will come to the evildoers in the end, although blood may be spilled before. I saw it in the cards yesterday, the day before." She was beginning to sound weak.

"I'll let you rest," Betty said. "You're going to be allowed to leave tomorrow. Do you want to come to my house? Just until you're completely well. Or you can stay with Miho. She's willing."

The eyes opened again, and Judit was smiling again. "I knew you would let me live in your house someday. The cards told me that too."

"Well, I'll come here after school tomorrow and drive you to whichever place you choose."

Betty knew, with a sinking feeling, that Judit would choose to live with her where she could take charge. Miho was probably too strong-willed to allow the old lady to take over her house.

"You are so good to me," Judit said. "I will come to you. It will be safer there, even if I have lost all my valuable jewelry."

Betty left her and drove back to her house, which would soon be filled with a card-reading old lady.

"You're going to have a new pal to bother," she told Tina, "and if I judge correctly, you'll be sorry." As much as Betty wanted to assist Judit, she was accustomed to being alone, to not sharing her bathroom, not having her meals at set times, to coming and going without having to think about another person. Perhaps Judit would soon find life on Timberhill Road tedious and choose to return to her

RV and her campfire at night. At least Betty had a refuge from her at the school.

Then she chided herself for her uncharitable thoughts. Of more concern was the possibility that Brad and Raven had stolen Judit's jewelry and gun. Then she had a chilling thought: Tommy, Brad's most ardent admirer, had been out late on his bike the night Judit was attacked. She prayed that he had not been party to that event, and had merely been riding away his grief at being refused by the girl he liked.

Then she pondered why Brad Melville would have written the excuse for tardiness yesterday morning. Surely he hadn't been at Tommy's house at the break of day. What had it said? *Important business to attend to.* That was Wednesday, her first day. The attack on Judit had come Wednesday night, after Betty's dinner at the Saks house. This morning, Thursday, Tommy had not come to school at all. We'll see if he comes tomorrow, she thought, and I'll visit the dress shop tomorrow about something to wear as a chaperon. Maybe Linda will have something to tell me. Then I'll bring Judit home in the afternoon. She wondered if Tommy would appear as scheduled on Saturday afternoon.

When she got home, Betty got a start on making up the little spare bedroom. She'd put up curtains when she first moved in, and there was a nice braided rug on the floor and a lamp beside the bed. All she needed to do was put sheets on the bed, and clear out a few things from the closet, so Judit would have room for her denim shirts and full, brightly colored skirts.

Then she called Miho to tell her that Judit would be staying with her for a time at Timberhill Road.

"Do not give her any rum," Miho said, "unless you want her to sing to you all night. She will probably cook for you," she added in an ominous voice, "but do not allow her to make a fire outside."

"She'll probably need to rest most of the time," Betty said. "She's an old lady who's been through a difficult experience. She can entertain the cat."

"She's good with plants," Miho said, "so she can look after the ones you bought from me. And if she is too much trouble, you can send her back here. Tell her that I really need her help with the vegetables."

"Thanks," Betty said. "She'll probably get pretty bored around here, and will want to get back to her RV and her campfire."

And Betty made a mental note to discuss this new situation with Ted. She called to make a date to see him tomorrow, after she'd investigated the possibility of a new dress and after Judit was settled in. She also wanted to discuss further the nature of Brad's attraction for the boys. And the robbery, the stolen gun, the stolen jewelry, and Brad's possible involvement. And Tommy's failed romance. All the surprising, unsettling things that appeared to be churning up the peaceful waters of East Moulton.

Betty did not sleep well that night. Her mind was too full of thoughts. Tina, however, sacked out at once, curled up on her feet, as though she'd genuinely missed Betty since she'd gone back to work.

CHAPTER 12

FRIDAY, END of the week with so much to do. Before she left for school, Betty took a quick look at her plantings in the backyard. It hadn't rained at all since she'd put the seedlings in the ground, and they were beginning to look a bit bedraggled. A few watering cans of water were necessary, and she drove away feeling that she had already fallen down on her job as a gardener. She'd find the garden hose which was somewhere in the basement near the monstrous black furnace and give them a good soaking that evening. Then she remembered. Judit would be there, she'd have to stop at the supermarket to buy groceries so they could have a quick bite before she went to see Ted as arranged, and she still had to look for a dress for the dance. She hadn't had so many tasks to accomplish since the old days.

She'd skip lunch, go to Town & Country, and beg Linda to pull the perfect answer to her clothing problem off the rack. She'd go to the supermarket, then bring Judit home and settle her in front of the TV set, heat something in the microwave, and when they'd finished eating, run across Timberhill Road to see Ted. It would all work out.

In this sudden flood of Things to Be Done, her easy retirement with a minimum of responsibilities took on a
rosier glow. Well, she'd be back to that soon enough.

The morning flew by. Marcy seemed a bit more cheerful
today, even though Tommy had shown up for school.
There was no sign or mention of Brad Melville, nobody
misbehaved severely enough to be sent to Sarah Carlson's
office, no angry parents called. At noon, she fled to the
Buick and drove to the town center and Town & Country
Fashions.

Linda Rockwell wasn't busy. In fact, the shop was
empty and she was sitting at the back of the shop near the
cash register reading the latest issue of *Vogue*. Professional advancement.

"Hello, Miss Trenka." At least she didn't sound angry
today.

"Hello, Linda. I need your help. That is, I need something to wear. I'm chaperoning the May Day dance tomorrow, and I literally don't have a thing to wear."

"I'm sure we can find you something. Although that
dance has caused me more trouble than it's probably
worth."

"I heard that Tommy took Marcy's rejection hard,"
Betty said. "It's not easy being young."

"He was devastated," Linda said. "Sarah Carlson called
me and suggested that we discuss sending Tommy to a
therapist. Not just because he didn't get a date with Marcy,
but other things. I talked it over with Joe, and he's ab-
solutely against the idea. Says there's nothing wrong with
his son, and he's not going to have the people in town
thinking Tommy is nuts, especially if he has to pay for it. I
know Tommy needs help, but I can't afford it without

Joe's help, and when Joe gets an idea in his head, there's no changing his mind." Linda looked so unhappy that Betty started looking through the dresses hanging on the racks herself. She didn't even want to suggest that there were ways to find low-cost help for someone like Tommy.

"Let me help you look," Linda said. "I think I know just the thing. The dress I sold to Raven would have been perfect for you, too. Youthful and elegant."

"Not exactly me," Betty said. "I'm more mature and sensible."

"How about this?" Linda pulled out a loose green satin jacket and a straight black skirt. "Very pretty with a nice string of beads or a lovely big pin. Not showy but tasteful. Accessories are so important these days."

Betty didn't know much about accessories, but she liked the green jacket, and the skirt looked simple and comfortable.

"I like it," Betty said, and she did have that nice jewelry that Sid had given her. The perfect accessories. She would almost imagine herself as a minor belle of the ball, dressed in the height of fashion.

"Don't take the first thing you see," Linda said. "Look around a bit while I make a phone call."

Betty didn't want to look anymore. She'd found what she needed, and she had to get back to her desk. But she glanced at a few racks while Linda spoke on the phone in a low voice. Betty was not the kind of person who eavesdropped, but she couldn't help noticing that Linda grew progressively more morose as the call went on, until she was nearly in tears by its end.

"Here, let me ring these up," Linda said. Now the tears were running steadily down her cheeks.

"What's wrong?" Betty asked, although she didn't expect Linda to give her any kind of definite answer.

"It's nothing, nothing," Linda said. "I'm just a fool." She totaled up the charges, and Betty handed her money. "I guess I shouldn't be taking a walk on the wild side at my age."

"Your age! Why, you're a kid compared to me," Betty said. "Is there anything I can do to help?"

Linda shook her head. "That was Joe, accusing me of having an affair with Brad Melville. Can you imagine? Just because I've had him over for dinner once or twice because Tommy asked me to invite him. Keep an eye on Tommy, Miss Trenka. I'm worried about him. He's been real depressed since this thing with Marcy. I'll see that he's at your place tomorrow morning, right on time."

"I think he said he was going somewhere with Brad in the morning," Betty said. "He said he'd be there in the afternoon." A little healthy exercise shooting rats and Tommy would be a lawn-mowing demon.

Then she thought, Shooting rats requires a gun. Where did Brad get a gun? She didn't like the answer that popped into her head. Then she thought, He's the kind who probably had one all along.

"Whatever," Linda said. She'd gotten over her upset, and now seemed indifferent to everything. Betty took her new clothes and left, to be back at school by the time the lunch hour ended.

The hospital told Betty that Judit would be discharged at four. She would just have enough time to see the school buses off and get to the hospital in time.

A final reprieve came just as school ended. Miho called to say that Judit had insisted that she return to her RV, not move in with Betty. "She can stay in my house for a day or two until she feels completely well," Miho said. "Then she can go back to living like the Gypsy she is."

"I didn't know if I would be able to handle having her with me," Betty said. "I hate to admit it, but I'm getting set in my ways. But please call on me if things get too difficult for you. I will fetch her from the hospital and bring her to you."

By six o'clock, Betty had delivered Judit to Miho's house, had shopped for groceries (for one instead of two, or two if you counted the cat), had checked again on her garden and found it thriving—or so it seemed to her eyes—and had changed into casual clothes to join Ted for a glass of wine before her microwaved dinner. Tina, of course, required her dinner at once, having nibbled on the dry food for far too many days, in her humble opinion.

"The blanc de blanc is nicely chilled," Ted called out when she rang his doorbell, heard "Enter," and walked into his handicapped-efficient home. "I wish you'd stay for dinner," he said. "I have some perfect king salmon that a friend caught in Alaska and had shipped to me flash frozen. A great fisherman."

"I'm almost too weary after this week to eat," Betty said. "I think I told you that Judit was going to be staying with me, but fortunately, she chose to return to the RV."

"Is she all right? I have only heard rumors about the break-in and robbery," Ted said as he poured the wine. "You have to tell me everything. And more. I suspect there is more."

"There is, and I need some advice, too," Betty said. "depending on how much you know about teenaged boys."

"Well, I was one, once. Drink up and we'll get to the serious stuff soon enough."

Betty began carefully, since she had her suspicions about Brad, and Brad was a strong right arm for Ted. First the details of the attack on Judit as she had heard them from Miho. Then a list of what had been stolen.

"I worry about the gun," she said. "And the possibility that your friend Brad Melville is involved." She explained about Judit's impression that one of the black-clad people had worn a silver chain and pendant.

"Sounds like Raven to me," Ted said, apparently unconcerned, "and if Raven was there, the other was likely Brad."

"That's what I thought," Betty said. "They've been to visit Judit before so Raven could ask her about magic, of all things. Judit never struck me as being involved in magic. On the other hand, she gave me a sketch of the curse she'd put on her grandsons if they were the culprits, and she sounded pretty convincing. Still, if she could do magic spells, and if they worked, she wouldn't be living in such dreadful circumstances."

"Maybe they're not dreadful to her. People's aspirations differ. What you and I consider dreadful may be perfectly fine to Judit."

"Did Brad come around to finish up with the hives?"

"Oh, yes. He was here, and the bees are fine. He worked very hard, and I think the garden is in good shape. Nothing to do now but pull weeds and give it a good soaking from time to time." Ted moved his wheelchair across the smooth wood floor to the windows that looked out on his garden in the back of the house. "We could use some rain, but the forecast is for more clear, fine weather for the next week, with only a slight chance for a shower tonight. I wish you'd ask Judit to send some rain." He turned the chair to face her. "Brad said or did nothing to indicate guilt for any action, if that's what you're waiting to hear me say. However, I put nothing beyond him, although he's never shown any criminal tendencies. I give him free access to this house, but nothing has ever gone missing. He's never crept in by night and taken anything, although there's quite a bit worth taking." He waved toward his wall of sound and computing equipment. "I think it's more likely that Judit's grandsons started feeling pinched and decided to liberate their grandmother's jewelry, although they won't get much for it."

"She swears it wasn't them," Betty said.

"But of course she would."

"And she won't talk to the police." Betty shrugged. "I guess that's an end to it, except for her missing gun."

They sipped wine in silence for a while. Then Ted said, "What do you need to ask about young boys?"

"It's Tommy Rockwell," she began, and Ted tilted his head questioningly. "You know, Penny Saks's nephew, the one who's coming on Saturday to mow my lawn." She'd already told him about her job at the school, and now explained how she'd heard about Tommy's rejection by Marcy, how he'd not come to school the next day, about the "excuse" from Brad, about his father Joe, and the hints that Joe had abused both Linda and Tommy, and now Joe was accusing Linda of being involved with Brad. Ted started to say something, then shook his head in a way to indicate that he didn't believe that at all.

"I didn't like hearing from one of the girls that Tommy had said he wished he were dead," Betty said. "Some of

the teachers suggest that he could use therapy to help with
his anger. I don't like the idea that he spends so much time
with Brad. Tomorrow, Brad's taking him to shoot rats at
the dump—one hopes not with the gun stolen from Judit."
And then she told him about chaperoning at the dance and
her plans to visit Sid Senior at the nursing home on
Sunday.

"A busy life for a retired lady," Ted said.

"Almost too busy," Betty said. "Although the school
job is a lifesaver. The principal is so nice, and the teachers,
too. Haven't had much to do with the children. Thankfully. Well, what do you think about Tommy?"

"He's probably troubled, but what teenager isn't? Life
seems impossible when you're that age, and the hormones
are raging and the girl of your dreams doesn't give you a
minute. Maybe some counseling by a professional would
help him, but I wouldn't worry about him too much. His
mother can handle him."

"I'm not so sure about that," Betty said. "Linda is pretty
shaky. Joe, her ex-husband, seems to be giving her grief
about Tommy, and about Brad, so she doesn't know where
to turn." Then she told him about seeing Linda's new beau
with Raven, and Phil's explanation of their long-term
friendship, and even Raven's snide remark at the dress
shop about Linda "stealing" a man. "Do you suppose she
thinks Linda has taken Phil away from her? I thought
Raven lived with Brad, and Phil's story doesn't sound as
though he dropped Raven for Linda."

"Maybe Linda should sit down for a long, sisterly chat
with Penny."

"And do what? Glue sequins on a pot? Mind you, I think
the world of Penny, but she might be just a bit too sunny to

understand Linda's problems. They're kind of dark. I wish I could be of help, but I just don't have the necessary experience in dealing with troubled children and difficult ex-husbands and jealous girlfriends. I suppose . . ." She stopped and stared at the ceiling.

"What are you supposing now, Elizabeth?"

"I was thinking that maybe I could talk with Tommy, tomorrow when he's at my house. Get him to express what's bothering him. Beyond girl problems, I mean."

"Kindly old grandmotherly Elizabeth?" Ted shrugged. "It might work, but my boyhood memories don't involve confiding in a woman half a century older than I."

"If I just had a clearer idea of what hold Brad Melville has over these kids. It's scary. Everyone says he's not a drug pusher, and they don't think he and Raven are sexual predators. I just don't understand what drives him."

"Hatred."

Betty stared at Ted. "What do you mean?"

"We've talked a bit, Brad and I, and from what I've heard, he's a very bitter young man. A bad childhood—no, wait, I'm not excusing him because he wasn't treated well here as a child. But he wasn't. A drunk for a father, a helpless mother. He thinks the town drove his father to drink himself to death, and then blamed him for the fire that destroyed the gas station. After he and his mother left town, she couldn't keep him, so he was passed from one relative to another, a frequent runaway, minor police trouble, and on and on, until he managed to get enough money to get away, get out of the country, and live by his wits all over the world. Adventures, and what now in the telling sounds like real excitement. But all that early stuff kind of soured him on human beings and especially the people of East

Moulton. He just hates everybody. He probably thinks that by filling these kids' heads with tall tales, he's liberating them early, teaching them to abandon their families, getting even. So they don't go through what he went through. So they'll be powerful enough to withstand what life throws at them. There, do I sound like a glib pop psychologist?"

"He scares me. Somebody else said he was out for revenge."

"That's the word I was looking for," Ted said. "He's doing it by playing with the minds of the town's kids."

"He still scares me," Betty said.

"He scares you because you think he can read your mind."

"Oh, I found out about that. He and Raven had just been to see Judit, who told them she had a pain and that I was her best friend. Nothing mysterious there. No, he's angry that I rejected the note he wrote for Tommy, and came pretty close to warning me that if I got in his way again, he'd handle me personally. But, Ted, I don't think boy liberation is a good enough reason for him to be allowed to gather all those kids to do his bidding. People say he takes a cut of the money the kids earn from the odd jobs he finds for them."

"Aha. He's a smart one. That's power—kidpower—a way to produce wealth, in a manner of speaking. No oil, no coal, no electricity, just muscle."

"In my opinion, that makes them slaves."

"Albeit willing ones. Look, Elizabeth, you can't stop Brad Melville from doing what he chooses. He's done nothing wrong, you have to admit that."

"No, but there *is* something wrong," Betty said stubbornly. "Raven scares me, too." She stood up. "I ought to be getting home. I have to be up early to organize my clothes for the dance and get ready for Tommy."

"The lawn mower is right inside the garage," Ted said. "Can you manage to get it across to your house, or do you want to send Tommy over for it tomorrow?"

"I can manage." Sometimes Betty liked to be as independent as Ted.

Ted opened the garage door for her from inside the house with his electronic door opener. Betty found the old manual lawn mower, dragged it across Timberhill Road, and leaned it against the side of her house near the back door. It was a relief to know she wouldn't have to be entertaining Judit as evening crept across the sky and the light faded. Just Betty and Tina, and the microwave.

Her new green satin jacket was on a hanger that she'd hooked on the mantelpiece near her retirement clock. It glowed in the lamplight. She held up the skirt and found that it was just the right length, no shortening required, fortunately. If she were not so tall, she would probably have had to get out needle and thread and clumsily try to sew a neat hem the way Ma had tried unsuccessfully to teach her to do years ago to get it to a proper length. Even if it wasn't exactly the most fashionable length, who was going to notice? No one who knew Elizabeth Trenka would care, and those who didn't know her wouldn't be paying any attention to her.

During the night, she was awakened by the sound of a gentle rain on her window. Good for the flowers, but the grass might be too wet to mow. Then she leaned back on her pillow and closed her eyes again. Tommy was coming in the afternoon, and if it was sunny tomorrow as promised, the damp grass would be dry by mowing time. It would probably grow even longer in the night.

She dreamed again of her pansies and petunias, sparkling with raindrops, and then, just before she awoke for the day, the dream showed her a figure standing in the shadows watching the flowers, nodding as if to music.

Very Walt Disney, she thought when she remembered the dream. Then she got up to greet a new day, not quite as filled with optimism as earlier in the week, but rather calm and satisfied.

CHAPTER 13

SHE AND Tina went outside after breakfast to view the patch of garden. All was well; she hadn't murdered one plant yet, and every one of them appeared to be thriving. She even picked a little bouquet of pansies for the kitchen windowsill. The grass was still wet from the night's rain, but she imagined how nice it would look neatly cropped and trimmed. She hoped that she could persuade Tommy to come every Saturday.

She strolled about her little domain, and considered how nice it would be to have a row of tomato plants in that sunny spot near the ruins of the old garage.

Consultation with Miho was in order, perhaps next week when she planned to visit Judit to see how she was recovering. Tomorrow she was driving north to see Sid Senior at the nursing home. Since his wife, Mary, had died he was as alone as Betty was. Well, he still had her, just as he'd had her beside him all those years at Edwards & Son. She'd tell him about her job at the school and perhaps even about Brad Melville and Raven. Even if his speech was impaired, Sid Senior seemed to enjoy listening to her talk and read the newspaper aloud. They'd been so close that she could usually tell what he was thinking or trying to say.

She paused to pinch a couple of dead petunia blossoms, and suddenly had a painful vision of young Tommy creeping through the town dump past piles of naked bedsprings and stepping over mounds of trash to take aim at a furry gray rodent. Would he have a rifle or a handgun? Before she could settle that, she imagined an explosion and the rodent flying through the air before crashing down lifeless on a pile of tin cans.

No, that wouldn't be right. East Moulton was dedicated to recycling. She herself dutifully put cans and bottles in a separate barrel, tied up newspapers, had a bag of recyclable white paper. The dump she was envisioning was an old one of her childhood, where everything was simply dumped: refrigerators, batteries, old chairs, garbage, everything. Still she could see in her imagination the bodies of rats shot by Tommy, Tommy himself proud of his aim, and beside him the silent figure of Brad Melville staring at the carnage with ivory and obsidian eyes. Was Raven sitting somewhere nearby in the car, examining her sharp red nails while her lover and his disciple slaughtered the hapless rats?

And did Betty imagine that Raven was smiling at the sight of blood and terror outside the vehicle? Did she smile when poor Judit was struck down and relieved of her gold chains?

Stop it! she told herself. You're doing too much imagining without the least basis in reality. Anyhow, the lure of the hunt appeared to be something males were enchanted by. Better rats than Bambi's mother, although Ted had extolled the virtues of well-cooked venison many times, and had even prepared a fabulous venison stew for her during the past winter, from game given to him by one of his hunting acquaintances.

Another sandwich for lunch, a change into old jeans, an older shirt, and scuffed and worn sneakers. She was going to be ready to pull dandelions and loosen the dirt around her plants while Tommy was pushing the mower back and forth across the grass.

Tommy appeared around one o'clock, pushing his bike up the driveway, and leaving it in the shade near the garage. Before she came out of the house, Tommy was testing the lawn mower, probably disappointed that it wasn't a big, powerful power mower. Unless she somehow acquired the empty field between her house and the Saks place, however, she wasn't eager to invest in equipment that wasn't really needed. It wasn't the money so much as she didn't want the responsibility of maintaining and harboring large mechanical objects.

"Hi, Tommy," she said from the back steps. "Maybe you should start here in back, while I pull a few dandelions in front. If I don't get them out before you mow, they'll just grow again."

That was probably some old story she'd heard from her mother, who didn't know what she was talking about since the Trenkas never had more than a four-foot square of grass in front of the two-family house where Betty had grown up and the strip of dirt where her mother had planted black-eyed Susans and sweetpeas every year. No! They were snapdragons, tall and stately, and there had been white daisies, too. Her grandmother, who had continued to live alone on the top floor of the house after Grandfather died, used to sit on a folding chair in the sun and give her mother advice in Czech, but Betty had never bothered to learn more than a few words of the language, so she didn't really know what her grandmother was saying. She might well have just been complaining about widowhood and the food shortages caused by the war, and saying nothing about a flower garden. In any event, Grandmother used to strip Ma's garden regularly so she could take flowers to Grandfather's grave, or give some to the sisters at the church where she attended mass daily until she was too old to walk. Betty suddenly noticed Tommy was looking at her puzzled.

"I was just thinking back to when I was your age," Betty said. "How was your morning?" She half-expected him to recount the stalking of rats through the trash at the dump. The excitement of the chase, the triumph of the hunter.

"Okay," Tommy said almost sadly, and Betty took a closer look at him. He seemed downcast, and didn't offer anything more, but simply started to push the mower in a straight line across the backyard, the grass falling to the turning blades. On the return trip, it seemed to Betty that his eyes were bright, but he seemed to be breathing heavily. She could already smell the scent of freshly mowed grass.

"Are you all right?" she asked, but he didn't answer. He seemed rather to be off in a world of his own. "If you get thirsty, I put some Cokes and stuff in the refrigerator. Help yourself."

"I don't want anything," Tommy said, and blinked rapidly. Good Lord, she thought, is he going to cry? Is he still depressed by Marcy's rebuff?

"Going to the dance tonight?" she asked brightly, but it

didn't seem to have much effect on his mood. "I'm going to be there as a chaperon."

Tommy stopped mowing in the middle of a row and looked at her. "I'll be there," he said. "You better believe I'll be there." He was expressionless as he spoke, but she sensed he was keeping control over his emotions. Whatever he was thinking, he wasn't going to share it with this old lady. "I got to show my power to . . . to all of those creeps. Brad says . . ." He stopped, and she never knew what Brad had said, but now she did see what looked like tears on his cheeks. He brushed them away quickly and went on with his mowing.

Betty was troubled by the suffering on his face and the anger in his voice. He was just a kid. Even to someone as inexperienced with children as she was, this clearly wasn't the way a kid should be feeling. Not on a pleasant Saturday afternoon with the sun shining and the prospect of a few dollars for a bit of simple labor.

"Don't feel too badly about the way things worked out," she said. "We all have our disappointments, even me, although you might not believe it. They hurt for a while, but life goes on. I can promise you that no matter how bad things seem now, it will go away."

"No," Tommy said as he resumed mowing. Then he called back over his shoulder, "Maybe it goes away if you've got the power to stop it." He paused. "Brad and I went up to the dump today, and man, is that place full of rats. Nobody likes them, so we got rid of a few. My mother almost wouldn't let me go, but Brad talked her into it. He said we were doing the town a favor, getting rid of pests. Like I'd like to get rid of some other pests. Raven said there have to be sacrifices, and she's smart, even smarter than Brad."

Hmm, the rats, the pests, got stopped, sacrificed. By a gun.

Betty didn't go around the front to pull weeds after all. She sat on the steps and watched the boy. She didn't like what she was hearing from him. He was troubled, but who was there to listen to him and ease those troubles? Not Brad Melville or Raven. She considered Raven. Maybe she was "smarter" than Brad. Betty had no way of knowing. But, perhaps influenced by Judit's premonition of an evil day, and the old lady's dislike of Raven, Betty wondered if she was filling Tommy's confused mind with ideas that weren't suitable. Sacrifices. Raven certainly wasn't referring to selfless surrender of personal desires to a greater good. No, there was a hint of ancient sacrifices, the snowy wings of doves splattered with blood.

Betty shook her head to chase away the images that suddenly filled her mind. She wasn't even sure the pictures of death that had come to her were products of her own mind, or if they were telling her of things to come. This was nothing she wanted to be part of. She didn't like feeling that she had foreseen something yet to be. An evil day.

Betty forcibly turned her thoughts back to Tommy. He needed something, somebody. His aunt Penny or uncle Greg? His mother? Even his father who watched football games with him and took him to sporting events? There had to be someone. Very likely Betty wouldn't be the right choice, and she hated to think that there was only Brad Melville that he'd talk to. It had to be someone in his family.

"I'll be right back," she said, and went into the house.

Linda Rockwell was listed in the slim East Moulton phone book, but there was no answer or answering machine when she called. Joseph Rockwell was listed too, but he was also not answering his phone.

Penny was home, but she was in the midst of spray-painting lawn furniture and couldn't run over to talk with her nephew. "Not just now, Betty. Maybe in an hour or two. I can't leave the painting in the middle of the job. It will dry funny. Greg isn't home; he and the Whiteys have gone off somewhere. Tommy's probably still upset about the dance. Yes, Linda told me about it. He was furious, said he'd get even, all kinds of nonsense. That awful Brad said it was always okay to get even, can you imagine?

"Look, if he still seems upset when he finishes mowing, send him over here. I'll stuff some cookies into him, and he'll be right as rain. And wasn't that rain last night wonderful? So good for my tomatoes, although the painting I did yesterday hasn't yet dried properly."

Betty listened for a few more minutes about Penny's arts and crafts and gardening triumphs and near-failures, then said, "I've got to run myself, Penny. By the way, where does Linda live? I mean, I might drive Tommy home, and I'd rather have directions in advance."

Linda and Tommy lived, it turned out, on one of the quiet roads off Main Street. Betty knew the street, with older houses that were kind of run-down. But there was a lot of space between neighbors and big old trees that looked as though they'd been around forever. A young woman she'd had an encounter with when she first moved to town had lived there, or a couple of streets over. She knew she could find it without any trouble.

Tommy had almost finished the backyard, so Betty finally went out front to dig up some dandelions. Tina followed her around to the front to play stalking beast in the tall grass. In a minute or two, Tommy pushed the mower around the corner of the house.

"You can start on this part," she said. "I've gotten most of the dandelions out." He just nodded. "I'd like to hear more about your adventure at the dump. It sounds like fun."

He stopped mowing, and a smile appeared (at last!).

"It was really great. Pow, pow, and if your aim is good, there's another one dead. And another." Now he sounded almost gleeful as he pantomimed shooting.

"I hope you were careful. Guns are dangerous."

"Brad knows all about them. It was a twenty-two pistol, a little gun. Brad's been a marksman for years and years. He says he always had to carry a gun when he was traveling over there. He said he'd take me again."

"And where did Brad get this gun?" Betty asked. She wondered if it was the one stolen from Judit. Of course, she had no idea what kind of gun Judit would have.

Tommy shrugged. "Somebody like Brad can get whatever he wants. I think he said it belonged to Raven." He looked slightly puzzled, as though he couldn't imagine why a mere girl would need a gun. " 'Course I know all about guns myself. My father has some, and he's taken me hunting lots of times. Squirrels and stuff. He said he'd buy me one of my own for Christmas. I'll be almost fifteen, that's old enough. Pow, pow."

She didn't care for the fact that he was aiming an imaginary pistol at poor Tina, who was gazing up at the blue spruce where some sparrows were having a confrontation, perhaps over the best location for a nest. He looked flushed with excitement now, but resumed mowing, moving slowly back and forth across the front lawn. It was quite hot, and Betty longed to get a cold soda or iced tea.

"I'm going to get something to drink," Betty said. "Care to join me?"

Tommy shook his head. "I'm nearly finished. Five, ten minutes more, then I'm going home. I got things to do there."

"I'll drive you, if you like. We could probably put your bike in the trunk." He shook his head again.

The lawn looked quite presentable at last, she thought as she stood on her front steps before going into the house. Before she got her drink, she went upstairs and found her handbag and the money she had agreed to pay Tommy. Then she found herself admiring the lawn from her bedroom window. The best thing was, she hadn't had to do it herself.

"It looks wonderful," she called down to Tommy. "I couldn't have done it without you. You're the best." She was pleased to see a big smile and a shy nod of his head. At least he seemed to have recovered from his earlier bout of sadness.

She almost missed his verbal response. "I'll do it every week, Miss Trenka. You're the best, too." That left her feeling oddly pleased. She couldn't have settled in a better place than happy, quiet East Moulton. Certainly the apartment complex where she'd lived near Hartford didn't have the pleasures of growing grass and smiling pansies, while it did have growing crime and grime, too many cars, too much traffic. Here she felt as though she'd returned to the peace of the upstate Connecticut town where she'd grown up.

She went out back again, to try to convince Tommy to let her drive him home, but Tommy and his bicycle were gone. Maybe he'd gone across to see Penny, or maybe he'd just pedaled on home. And he hadn't waited to be paid.

CHAPTER 14

BETTY WENT in to the cool dimness of her living room and sat on the sofa.

The prospect of being a chaperon in a few hours' time was giving her a slightly nervous feeling in the pit of her stomach. And the more she thought about it, the more uneasy she felt about the very unnerving hints that Tommy had given. Hadn't anyone else heard him and understood?

Was he really thinking of getting even with the girl who had turned him down? And thinking it was right to do so because Brad had said it was? That it was a good deed to get rid of "pests"? She didn't like this business one bit, but there was no one she could turn to.

Well, there was one person who had to be responsible for the boy. She'd get ready for the evening early and drive to Linda Rockwell's house. With luck Tommy would not have left for the May Day dance. She'd make Linda understand, and then the two of them could talk some sense into him. She had read too many news stories of boys turning on their classmates because they were hurt or angry. That certainly described Tommy. He wanted to get even, and he had the revenge-bent Brad as his mentor, a man who always had a gun, whose coterie of boys did his bidding. Betty sighed. It might all be in her own imagination, but she'd have to handle it. Personally.

Certainly she had the perfect excuse for showing up at Tommy's house. She owed him money for his work, and he might need it for a soda after the dance, if he managed to join a friendly group of classmates. And if he didn't . . .

Suddenly East Moulton's peace seemed false, a cheerful façade that disguised a crueler reality.

Betty took a long bath to wash away the dirt from her lawn work, then washed her long, heavy hair, blew it dry with her sturdy hair dryer (a long, tedious task) and carefully fashioned it into a rather elegant bun on the nape of her neck.

As she donned her new clothes and chose one of the jeweled brooches Sid had bought for her on his travels, she felt almost as if she were getting ready for a date to take her to the dance, and she should be peeking out the window to see if he'd driven up yet. She did peek out the window, and saw that the light was beginning to fail, but all she noticed were some lights in Ted's house behind the trees. She hoped that she would see Tommy on his bike returning to get paid, but the road was empty.

She wished Tommy knew Ted and had him to talk to instead of Brad Melville. Ted had faced much worse than female rejection and teasing of schoolmates, and yet had managed to cope with life in an amazingly positive way.

She had half a notion to go over and ask Ted what to do about her concerns about Tommy that she'd only skirted earlier, but now that was out of the question. Time was short, and she had to get going.

She'd drive to Linda's house. The dance was to start at eight, so if she reached Linda's by seven-thirty, she'd be away in time to climb on her chaperon's pedestal in the school gym as the music started. Then she couldn't remember when things started. Was it seven or eight? She ought to know; she'd typed the time in the bulletin. Her fading memory again. Maybe everyone would be fashionably late, so it wouldn't matter when she arrived. Cindy had told her there would only be recorded music, no band—that was a perk reserved for the senior prom.

"There's a guy who's a pretty good disc jockey. He works regularly at one of the clubs up at the mall," Cindy had said. "The kids like him, and we teachers can make him turn down the volume for a time when it's more than our aging ears can stand. It's mostly pretty loud music, I'm afraid. The kids aren't really big on slow romantic dances. Don't look so alarmed, Betty. He always throws in a few old tunes for the old-timers. Larry can spin you around the floor to one of those."

Since she was ready with nothing to do, she tried calling Linda again, and again there was no answer. Surely Tommy would have had time to ride home by now. Or maybe because Tommy had decided to go to the dance solo, Linda was prettying herself up for a date with Phil Rice.

She paced for a while, but couldn't shake her uneasiness. Finally she called Ted, who said, yes, he'd be at home all evening.

"I might need to call on you for more advice," Betty said. "Nothing significant."

"I need something less tantalizing than that to keep me happy," Ted said. "What's troubling you? Something is. I can hear it in your voice."

"I . . . I'm afraid something bad is going to happen. Just a feeling I have," Betty said. "Tommy Rockwell is being egged on by Brad, I'm sure of it. To do something, to get even. Brad's revenge on East Moulton through a little boy. But it's still just a premonition."

"Well, call me if you need me. Remember how Raven's mind reading worked out. Perfectly logical reason for her to know something. I'll bet your premonitions are just the same."

"Yes," Betty said slowly. "There are perfectly logical reasons. That's what worries me."

She carefully applied a minimum of makeup, as she didn't consider herself the type for mascara, eyeliner, and carefully lined lips. Then she got into her trusty Buick and drove along Timberhill Road toward the center of town. She found Linda's street without trouble and even found her house quickly. She frowned. Tommy must have already departed for the dance because the house was dark, except for a light behind the curtains on the second floor. She hoped she wouldn't be disturbing a romantic episode between Linda and Phil.

The houses on either side of Linda's house were also completely dark, and mostly hidden behind aggressively private hedges and trees. There were no cars parked along the sides of the street, no sounds of television from any of the scattered houses.

Linda's place was a sprawling, old-fashioned house, with a sagging veranda boasting a few bits of wicker furniture. Unlike her own, the lawn wasn't freshly mowed. Tommy obviously didn't have that chore at home. The windows into the dark living room were covered with transparent white curtains, but when Betty peered in, she didn't see anything but furniture shapes, and nobody answered the doorbell, which Betty could hear bonging somewhere inside.

She tried the doorknob tentatively and found that the door opened readily. When she poked her head in, all she noticed was the silence, and the faint sound of a faucet dripping into water, probably in the kitchen at the back of the house.

"Hello? Tommy, are you here?" But there was no answer. "Linda? It's Elizabeth Trenka." Still no answer, and now she sniffed. Some faint and unfamiliar odor hung in the warmish air. Sickly and unpleasant. And another, sharper scent, almost chemical in nature. Betty hesitated. She couldn't simply walk into another person's house without a good reason, with no reason at all for that matter. She wouldn't go very far in, just far enough to turn on the standing lamp she saw silhouetted against the near wall. The sudden bright light showed her an ordinary living room: a sofa upholstered in plaid and a matching loveseat, a low coffee table with a pile of magazines, wooden floors with colorful area rugs. A flight of stairs carpeted in beige led to the second floor, and beyond the living room, she could see a dining room and the corner of the kitchen.

"Hello?" she called again, and this time she thought she heard a response from above, not words, but a low moan. She must be mistaken. The absolute silence returned.

I am getting as nosy as the rest of the town, she thought, as she made the decision to go upstairs to see what was there. She stopped at the foot of the stairs. The light-colored carpeting was soiled. It looked like a footprint, as though someone had stepped in something and had marked the rug upon descending. She touched the spot with one finger. It felt dampish, and on her finger was a reddish brown residue. Her first thought was that it was blood, and a sudden clutch of fear hit her in the stomach. Then she hurried up the stairs, taking care not to touch the brownish footprints that appeared on almost every riser, nor to touch the walls or banister.

"Linda! Tommy!" She could hear the fear in her voice. At the top of the stairs, she stopped. She was certain she had heard the sound of a flimsy door slamming shut. It couldn't have been the front door where she'd entered because she could look back down the stairs and see it. The back door from the kitchen then. She immediately turned toward the half-open door to the room where the light was on, and approached it cautiously. She'd worry later about who'd left the house just now.

She was never to forget the horror that lay before her. Linda Rockwell was sprawled on the bed on her back, her chest covered with blood. There was blood on the pillows and sheets. Bloody fingerprints on the white headboard. From the doorway, it seemed to Betty that there was a gaping wound in her chest—a gunshot? Stabbing? There was blood on the floor, and more of those footprints where someone had stepped in the gore and walked away.

Very carefully, she approached the bed and took Linda's wrist to feel for a pulse. There was none. Linda's dying moan must have been what she'd heard downstairs. She felt for a pulse on her neck but found no sign of life there either. She took a deep breath but was not calmed. Had it been the murderer who had slammed the door? Where was Tommy?

The thought of Tommy gave her pause. She had seen in her mind bodies of dead and dying children, as a slight boy with a gun took aim at them as though they were just so many rats at the dump. She hadn't dreamed that she would find a hardworking, pretty young woman lying in her own blood in her own house.

If Linda had just been shot, she had heard nothing. Maybe the neighbors had heard a shot, even though their houses were some distance from this one. The first thing she must do is get help, and then go on to find Tommy before more terrible things happened.

There was a telephone beside the bed, but Betty hesitated to touch it. She'd read enough mysteries and watched enough TV to know that the police checked everything for fingerprints. Finally she took a clean handkerchief from her handbag, used it to lift the receiver, and telephoned the resident state trooper.

He answered promptly.

"Officer Bob, it's Betty Trenka. I need you. I mean, someone's dead. Shot, I think." She was beginning to breathe hard, and she felt a wave of hysteria rising. No, no hysterics for Elizabeth Trenka. She got a grip on herself, and explained where she was and who was dead. The resident state trooper knew Betty well from an earlier deadly affair just after she'd moved to town. "I tried to find a pulse, there wasn't any, but she might still be alive. Hurry."

"I'm on my way," Bob said. "Do you know who did it, Miss Trenka?"

"No," Betty said. She couldn't just blurt out Tommy's name. She couldn't believe he was responsible for killing his own mother, just because he'd seemed alternately elated and depressed this afternoon. She didn't know if he'd done this to Linda, or whether there could be another who wanted her dead. Linda was so pleasant and ordinary, not an obvious victim. Then she remembered that strange and terrible things went on behind the pleasant and ordinary lives one saw everyday. "I can't wait here for you. I have to leave. It's very important. I work at the school, and they're expecting me. I mean, I have to help a friend in trouble." She shuddered at her vision of the trouble looming.

"Can you write down where you'll be, how we can find you? Then run along to the school. I'll be there as soon as I can."

Betty sat down in the little straight chair in the hallway outside of Linda's room to calm her nerves. She looked at her watch. She should have been at the school by now. But these were extraordinary circumstances, so she could be forgiven for being late. But what about Tommy? He'd spun out some threats of revenge; he was going to the dance. If blood lust was raging through his adolescent veins, there could be worse things in store. She had to find him right away. She had to be in time.

Carefully she wrote out a note to Officer Bob, saying exactly where she could be found, and why, and placed it on the floor, squarely in front of the door to Linda's room, where he couldn't miss it. Then she went downstairs again, touching nothing, and drove somewhat shakily to the East Moulton school.

She could see the lights on in the school. The parking lot had quite a few cars in it. Almost everyone should be there by now. She wondered if Tommy had ridden over on his bike, or whether he was hiding somewhere in the throes of grief. She didn't want to think that he had been responsible for the awful bloody body she'd seen, but it was hard to get around that possibility. If he had done it, he must be in a terrible state, capable of doing even worse, if anything could be worse.

As she turned into the parking lot, and as the headlights swept the stairs into the building, she saw a slight figure on the steps. If it was Tommy—it looked like him—she might still be in time.

Betty pulled into the first open space she came to and quickly got out of the car. She wasn't much for running, but she moved as fast as she could toward the school.

The boy was wearing a backpack, and he had on a blue blazer and gray trousers. She didn't want to call out to him or alarm him in any way. Then as he opened the big door into the school, she saw his face in the light. Tommy.

His face was white and his expression dazed. He walked into the building, and Betty followed, close on his heels.

Tommy stood at the end of the long corridor as though listening to the music coming from the gymnasium at the end of the hallway. Betty noticed that somebody had draped the doorway to the gym with multicolored ribbons and bunches of spring flowers. Decorations for May Day.

Mayday. That's a phrase from my youth, Betty thought, when the news was full of the war in Europe and the Pacific. Mayday was a military distress call. Help me.

She watched Tommy walk slowly toward the big room full of dancing couples, a slight, dejected figure, someone who needed help. It was as if the boy, the whole building, was screaming *Mayday*.

Betty approached Tommy quietly, and said, "I can help you if you'll let me. I'm a little late, but I know all about it. Let me help."

Tommy turned to her eagerly.

"You left before I could pay you," Betty said. "So I went to your house, in case you needed the money for the dance. I called the police."

A frightened look appeared on his face.

"My mother," he said. "I found her when I got home. I . . . I didn't know what to do, so I changed my clothes and I left. I rode my bike here. Miss Trenka, I feel like I'm dying, like we're all dying." His voice broke, and tears rolled down his cheeks.

"Did you hurt your mother?" Betty asked.

"No!" He started to reach around to his backpack.

"Let me just take that, it doesn't look proper for a school dance."

He pulled away from her, and slipped off the backpack, cradling it in his arms. "I need it. I need it to get even." He sounded desperate.

"Getting even doesn't always work," Betty said. "Getting even has consequences that aren't pleasant."

Betty thought that the discovery of his murdered mother was enough to upset any teenaged boy. Because he was upset didn't necessarily mean that he had harmed her, but he might well be upset because of what he planned to do.

"Tommy, the police will be coming here soon. The least you can do is tell me what you planned to do here, tell me what happened at home, and give me that backpack. I won't open it, but it might not be a good idea for you to be holding it when they show up."

The tension seemed to drain away from him, but he kept holding the backpack.

"I didn't hurt Mom," he said, "but I want to hurt somebody. Whoever hurt her. She's . . . she's dead, isn't she? I want to hurt everyone who's ever hurt us."

"Not Marcy, I hope," Betty said.

He wrinkled his nose. "Not her. I used to like her, but she's just a dumb girl. But sometimes today I thought about blowing them all away like the rats at the dump."

"I rather thought so. What else? What happened when you got home?"

"I told you. I saw Mom lying there, but I was pretty sure she was dead. I could tell just by looking at her. Someone came into our house before I got home and shot her." He looked at Betty as he processed that thought. "Who would do that? Then I just got so mad I wanted to punish everybody. I wanted them all dead." Betty could hear the edge of hysteria in his voice and was afraid he was going to break down in front of her. Better that than a roomful of dead children.

"Did you see anyone, anything?" Betty reached out her hand, but he still refused to hand over the backpack.

"No. No one was around. The door is always unlocked, so anyone could have come in. For a minute when I was upstairs, I could see down the stairs and I thought I saw . . . somebody near the door, but then I went to Mom, and . . . and . . ."

A whole list of people flashed through Betty's mind. Phil Rice. But what reason would he have to kill Linda? Joe Rockwell. If he was as violent as reported, maybe he didn't need a reason to kill his former wife. Troubled Tommy was always a possibility, but she was beginning to doubt that he could have done it. The only people left to her knowledge were Brad and Raven, but they too had no reason to commit such a crime. Even if they had attacked Judit and were responsible for stealing her jewelry, there had been no indication that Linda Rockwell's house had been ransacked by robbers after she had been shot. But if they wanted revenge on the town, what better way than to urge on someone like Tommy to commit a grave crime that would affect everyone in East Moulton.

"Look who's here," said a voice behind them. Betty turned and saw Raven in her floating black silk shirtwaist, with the gleaming silver skull at her throat, and Brad looking remarkably put-together in a decent black jacket and trousers.

"How's it going, kid?" Brad punched Tommy on the shoulder. Then he peered into the gym where the DJ was spinning records, and almost everyone seemed to be dancing. "Nice little pack of rats in there."

"Mmmm." Tommy looked a little scared.

"Go for it, kid. Power, remember. You have the power now. Be strong." Brad took Raven's elbow and escorted her into the dance. Raven looked back over her shoulder at Betty and smiled the most malevolent smile she'd ever seen. Evil day, evil woman.

"What did he mean?" Betty asked, almost willing herself not to understand. "What is he doing here? This is a dance for the schoolkids, not adults." She scanned the room to see if she could locate Larry or Sarah Carlson to have Brad removed. Still, the police would soon be here to speak to her and Tommy. She trusted Officer Bob to be true to his word. She had relied on him before and not been disappointed.

Tommy said, "It's just something we talked about before, when he came to pick me up to go to the dump. Mom . . ." His voice broke, but he got control quickly. "She didn't want me to go, she called Raven bad names, and Brad, too. Raven really gave it to her then. But I went anyhow. She can't keep me from doing what I want." Defiant now, but then he remembered.

Mom couldn't keep him from doing anything, not anymore.

CHAPTER 15

Tommy CALMED down a bit, but still looked pale and scared. And he still had his backpack in his arms. Betty watched him edge toward the door to the gym, as though keeping track of Brad and Raven. She followed him and looked over his shoulder. When he found them standing to the side chatting, she felt his body tense.

"Don't even think about going in," Betty said. "We have to wait for Officer Bob." Just then she saw Raven go onto the dance floor with Larry. True to his word, he did dance with the ladies.

"Tommy, I have to go into the dance to tell Mrs. Harris that I'm here, but I want you to stay right where you are and do nothing. Understand? Nothing. No getting even, no showing how much power you have."

He didn't answer her.

Betty looked around for someone to stay with him while she attended to her responsibilities. The only person she saw nearby was Brad, who was watching Raven as he stood with his back to the wall. Then he caught her eye and walked over.

"Tommy is a little upset," Betty said. Brad nodded.

"The police will be here shortly," she added. "I don't know if you know what's happened."

Brad gazed at her, expressionless. Then she saw Sarah Carlson and waved to get her attention. Sarah approached through the mass of dancing teenagers, and Betty took her aside.

"Something terrible has happened," she said, and explained briefly about Linda Rockwell. "I don't know if Tommy was involved in any way, but I don't want to leave him here alone with . . ." She noticed that Brad was leaning down talking to Tommy, who wore a rather grim smile.

"How awful! We must call the police," Sarah said.

"They were called and should be arriving shortly," Betty said. "I wanted to tell Cindy that I was here, if not at my post."

"Don't worry about that," Sarah said. "Poor Tommy." Then she glanced at Betty with a look of horror as what Betty had told her sank in. "Did he do it? Shoot his mother? Oh, Lord, what have our children come to? I can't believe that he'd do such a thing. And how? Guns aren't common among the kids here. There's a bit of hunting done, so there are those weapons around town. Maybe we should take him to the office, get him away from all this."

"Good idea," Betty said. "I think I must call Linda's sister, Penny Saks, to let her know what's happened. And his father. Then the police will want to talk to Tommy away from everyone."

Sarah said, "If it wasn't Tommy, and I pray it wasn't, could it have been Joe Rockwell? That temper of his . . ."

"We don't know anything," Betty said, and saw that Raven had divested herself of Larry and was standing with

Brad, both watching Betty and Tommy. "Come along, Tommy." She took his arm, but Tommy pulled away from her grasp.

"No," he said quite calmly. "I want to see someone in there."

"I'm afraid you can't, not just now."

"I got to talk to Brad," he said, and there was an edge of hysteria in his voice. "And Raven. Especially Raven."

Raven looked around quickly at the sound of her name. The wicked, superior smile was still there, and she boldly waved her crimson-tipped hand to him.

"Later," Betty said, "when we've cleared things up."

"No," Tommy said. "Now. I'll clear things up myself." He moved away from Betty and fumbled with the zipper on the backpack. It happened quickly, but Betty saw the gun in his hand, and he was pointing it at Raven, who stared back at him with her mouth open. Behind Raven were a hundred dancing children, including Tommy's lost love, Marcy, Cindy Harris with a man who was probably her husband, Denise, and Kevin. Larry dancing with an older woman—Miss Novak of all people. All of them in Tommy's line of fire.

Betty wasn't sure her aging legs would carry her very quickly across the short space between her and Tommy, but Sarah seemed immobilized, and Raven and Brad weren't moving at all. Betty sprinted, and caught the arm holding the gun from below, so that when the shot was fired, the bullet sped toward the ceiling of the gym where crepe paper streamers and balloons hung from the rafters.

He managed two wild shots, and he and Betty fell in a heap at Raven's feet as some balloons popped and a shower of ceiling debris and streamers fell about them.

The screams of the children must have penetrated the brain of the disc jockey, because he quickly switched from the loud rock tune that had been playing to a soothing Frank Sinatra song.

Betty scrambled to her feet in time to see Brad and Raven hurrying down the hall toward the exit. Sarah Carlson stood beside her with her arms raised.

"Nothing to worry about," she said in a commanding voice. "Just an accident. Keep on dancing. Mr. McGovern is in charge." Larry looked bewildered, but nodded, and then steered Miss Novak around the floor to the tune of "My Way." Then to Betty, Sarah said, "Let's get Tommy out of here." They grasped his arms and pulled him to his feet. Betty took the gun from his limp hand and managed to guide him to the office, where she unlocked the door, leaving Sarah to meet the police when they arrived and bring them in to Tommy.

Tommy sat in one of the chairs near the door, still clutching the backpack.

"Here, now you can let me take that," Betty said. "It's best you aren't holding it when Officer Bob gets here."

Now he did relinquish it, and she put it on the desk while she called Penny. Someone had to. The conversation was difficult, but it so happened that a state trooper had already visited the Saks house with the news of Linda's murder. Betty was glad she didn't have to be the one to tell her what had happened.

"Who could have done it?" Penny wept into the phone. "It's unbelievable. Linda. Who would kill Linda?" She paused. "Joe. Or her new boyfriend. I don't know much about him, but I've always thought Joe was a little unbalanced. But not to the point of this."

"No one knows yet. At least I don't. But I have Tommy here with me at the school. Apparently he came home and found his mother, then left again for the dance." She decided against telling Penny that Tommy had a gun when he got to the dance. "I went to Linda's house to pay Tommy what I owed him, and I was the second to find her. I called the police and got to the school as fast as I could, in case . . ."

"In case what?" Penny asked.

"I was afraid . . . afraid that Tommy might do something foolish."

"What do you mean?"

"I wasn't sure whether Tommy had shot his mother, and if he had a gun, I was worried that he might try to harm the students, get even for being rejected, lash out because his mother had been murdered. Or something."

"Shall I come to the school?" Penny asked. "Where's his father?"

"I haven't tried to reach him yet, although I called him this afternoon, but got no answer. It might be a good idea if you or Greg were here at least. I wouldn't want the police questioning him without a family member present."

"Question him? Why? Just because he was traumatized by finding his mother dead?"

"It's possible," Betty said, "that they may think he did it."

"That's ridiculous. Where would Tommy get a gun to shoot anybody?"

"A gun was stolen from old Judit a few days ago. It seems likely that Brad and Raven had something to do with that. Brad had a gun to take Tommy to the dump to shoot rats just this morning. Take my word for it, there's a gun around, and Tommy had it."

"Greg or I will be right there," Penny said. "Somebody has to stay here with the Whiteys."

Sarah came into the office. "They're pretty much calmed down," she said. "But there's a lot of talk. Several of the kids saw Tommy with the gun. Where's it got to?"

"I have it here," Betty said. "Brad and Raven made a hasty departure."

"Was he really trying to shoot his classmates?"

"Were you, Tommy?" Betty asked the dazed boy sitting in the chair where he usually sat when he got sent to the principal's office.

He shook his head. "I don't know. Brad says you got to get even, and if you hurt them, they know you've gotten even with them. Raven calls it a sacrifice to clean away the bad stuff. But . . . but . . . she never said she'd do bad stuff to me." The tears began to flow again.

"Tommy," Betty said gently, "when you found your mother, did you also see Raven near your house?"

He nodded. "She was outside on the veranda waiting for me. She was supposed to give me the gun. I put it in my backpack. Then Phil came by to pick up Mom, but Raven told him that my mother was sick and couldn't go out tonight. She went away and I changed my clothes and went in to see Mom. That's when I . . . I found her. I went downstairs, and I was in the kitchen when I heard you come in, so I left."

"Out the back door. I heard it slam," Betty said. "It's going to be all right, Tommy. Your aunt Penny will be here soon." And the police, she hoped. Somebody had to find Raven and Brad.

Suddenly the school office was full of large people in uniform, and she was relieved to see Officer Bob, looking as handsome and competent as ever. She saw two of the town constables, and then Penny, who rushed over to hug Tommy.

"Miss Trenka, I understand that you're the heroine in this terrific mess," Officer Bob said. "They're saying this young fellow tried to shoot some people at the dance, and you knocked the gun away."

"One does what one must," Betty said. "If it hadn't been me, one of the other adults would have tried to stop him. But I'm not convinced he was going to shoot the kids, just Raven. A matter of getting even."

"There's the matter of his mother's murder," the officer said.

"Raven again, I think," Betty said. "A sacrifice."

"You're going to have to explain that," he said. "Now I ought to talk to the lad while everything is clear in his mind."

"His aunt is here," Betty said. "I don't know where his father is."

"Joe Rockwell is being questioned elsewhere." When Betty looked startled, he added, "A woman gets murdered, we sort of automatically take a look at spouses and ex-spouses. Especially those with reputations for flying off the handle. No definite reason to believe he had anything to do with it."

"I suggest you find Raven," Betty said stubbornly. "And Brad Melville."

"I'll trust you on that," the policeman said, and gave instructions to one of the constables to locate Brad.

Officer Bob took Tommy and Penny aside to talk, and

Betty sat wearily at her desk. The computer's dark eye reminded her that things would be different when she returned to work on Monday. Then she thought that nobody
was going to find Brad Melville at home, wherever that
home might be. He and Raven wouldn't be so foolish as
simply to retire to their place of residence and wait to see
what happened, especially if they were parties to the death
and destruction that had marked this May Day night.

CHAPTER 16

AFTER BETTY had reported her part in the affair and explained why she had felt that Tommy might do something destructive, she was dismissed. When she was certain that Tommy was only in trouble for bringing a gun to the dance and was not seriously suspected of murdering his mother, she asked Sarah if she could leave.

"I hate not to live up to my obligations as a chaperon," Betty said, "but it has been a difficult evening."

"We'll manage without you," Sarah said. "We may even close down the dance early under the circumstances. I don't want an endless stream of telephone calls from complaining parents about keeping them here when it could be dangerous. And, Betty, it's thanks to you that we didn't have a terrible tragedy tonight. It was very wise of you to see the danger when none of the rest of us did, and then to prevent anything from happening. The whole town will be grateful to you when the news gets out."

"I'd rather it didn't," Betty said, but she knew that as soon as Molly picked up a hint of what had happened, she'd find out every detail, and if she couldn't, she'd make up her own and share everything from one end of East Moulton to the other.

"I hope you get some rest," Sarah said.

Penny, still red-eyed from crying, said before she left with Tommy, "Greg and I will do what we can to get custody of Tommy. Joe and his wife don't really want him." At least Tommy had a familiar place to spend the night, and Betty was sure that he'd retire tonight stuffed with cookies and warm milk. As he walked toward the office door, Tommy stopped beside Betty.

"You're smart, Miss Trenka, smarter than Raven."

"I'm sorry about your mother, Tommy. Come see me any time if you need to talk to somebody. And wait, I still haven't paid you for your work." She found the money she'd set aside for him in her handbag and added an extra five-dollar bill. "I'll see you whenever you feel like mowing again." She watched him be taken off with his aunt, half an orphan, and with luck, not to be handed over to the full custody of his abusive father.

She straightened her green satin jacket, made sure Sid's brooch was still safely pinned to the collar, and nodded her good-nights to the crowd still in the office.

The sound of music from the dance echoed along the corridor, but here and there, parents who had arrived to carry their children off to the safety of home were frantically scurrying away. Word traveled fast in East Moulton, and news like this had probably wakened Molly from a sound sleep to spread the word.

"Miss Trenka . . ." It was one of the parents of a boy in the library reading group. "What happened here tonight? I got word there was a shooting, but nobody seems to know just what went on."

"It was nothing," Betty said. "A prank that went a bit wrong. Nobody was hurt. Don't worry."

Then Marcy caught up with her at the door. "I saw Tommy looking at me," she said. "I'll never forget his expression. He . . . he would have shot me if it hadn't been for you. I know it. Just because I didn't want to go to the stupid dance with him. That makes it my fault."

"It was more than that, Marcy. And it's not your fault. We're responsible for our own actions, and Tommy is responsible for what he did, what he planned to do. He's suffering now, because someone murdered his mother, so try to be kind to him, even if you don't want to go on a date with him."

"His mother was *murdered*? I didn't hear that."

"You will, and people are going to say that he did it, but I don't think he did."

"Probably that creep Brad, if you ask me."

"And if you ask me," Betty said. "Good night, Marcy. Tomorrow will be a better day. It always is."

When Betty was seated in her car, she couldn't shake the feeling that there was unfinished business to attend to. She hated not having all the loose ends tied up.

The only loose ends she could see were Brad and Raven. Before she left the office, Officer Bob had told her that the constable hadn't found Brad and Raven at the shack they rented, and it appeared that they had gathered up their things and left hastily.

"Shouldn't be too hard to locate them soon," Officer Bob said. "They're kind of distinctive characters."

Betty continued to sit in the Buick while a steady stream of cars left the parking lot. Where would Brad and Raven go? Probably as far away from East Moulton as possible, and as quickly as possible. She should just allow the authorities to find them and to piece together any evidence that might show that Raven had murdered Linda Rockwell. Had sacrificed her to drive Tommy to do as much damage to as possible, ensuring that he'd have a weapon to inflict death on his classmates. But somehow Tommy had understood, and he'd attempted instead to use the gun on Raven.

So I saved her life, Betty thought. I suppose I can't expect her to be grateful.

She sighed. It was still fairly early. Suddenly she had a sense of seeing Raven somewhere in the warm night. May Day. Sitting somewhere so that the light of a fire danced across her high cheekbones and glinted off her red nails. Betty started the engine, and pulled out of the parking lot. She drove along a quiet Main Street, with only the streetlights to show the closed shops. Even the pharmacy was closed. Molly was probably broadcasting from her home telephone. She turned left at the stoplight and drove toward Miho's house. She was certain she'd find Raven sitting with Judit at the campfire, plying her with rum and trying to learn a magic spell to protect her from pursuit and justice. At night, the way to the greenhouse was dark and closed in by the trees growing close to the road. There were no other cars on the road, and no streetlights here away from the center of town.

As she approached Miho's house, she saw there were one or two lights on, but the greenhouse was dark except for a dim night-light that shone faintly through the glass walls and roof.

On the other side of the house, though, she saw the dancing flames of Judit's fire, and the lumpish shape of Judit herself, who appeared to be dozing in the lounge chair. No car, no sign of Raven having her cards read by firelight.

Betty pulled into the dirt drive and got out. Judit did not stir, and Betty worried briefly that she had been assaulted again. No, Judit was snoring peacefully, wrapped in a blanket. There was only a small bandage covering the spot where she'd been attacked earlier.

"Judit," Betty whispered and shook her gently. After a moment, Judit opened her eyes, which were full of fear and confusion. "It's me, Elizabeth. Are you all right?"

Judit managed to sit up and shake away sleep before focusing on Betty, who caught a whiff of alcohol.

"Elizabeth, what are you doing here?"

"Maybe you should go inside to sleep," Betty said. "The damp night air can't be good for you. You just got home from the hospital. Have you been out here alone all evening?"

Betty's eyes widened as the blanket fell away from Judit's chest and she saw the gleam of a gold necklace around her neck. "Where did you get that?"

"An old lady can only answer one question at a time," Judit said. "I have been here since the sun went down. I don't know what the time is now. When you say 'that,' what is it that you mean?"

"Your necklace. You got it back?"

"Only one," Judit said. "The others, I think I will never see again. The one from when my first son was born, the one from the second. This is from the third. The earrings my husband bought me when the first grandson was born. And on and on."

"But where did you get it this time?"

"The bad 'un brought it to me. Tonight, not long ago.

The black bird came with the man and we drank beside the fire for a time. Then she gave me the necklace because she said she knew now that she was powerful and she didn't need my trinket. She had me read her cards and listened well, although the man would not listen."

"And what did her cards say?" Betty wondered how she had known that Raven would seek out Judit.

"Death was there, death in the past and in the future. That pleased her, although it does not please me to foretell death. And then there was something I saw that troubled me greatly. It had to do with you, Elizabeth."

Judit started to hum to herself, and Betty wanted to shake her so she would tell her what she meant.

"She is burning up with the desire for revenge," Judit said at last. "How have you harmed her?"

"I haven't harmed her. She's done everything to herself."

"But I saw blood," Judit said. "And I was afraid it was yours. I do not wish harm to come to my friend." Now she started to sniffle a bit, imagining danger to Betty.

"Well, I'm here and I'm all right," Betty said. "I have had a difficult time tonight, but all the blood is over with. Here, get up and go to sleep inside your RV. Weren't you going to stay in Miho's house for a few days?"

"I do not like the smell of fish," Judit said, "and I don't like the box with pictures and people laughing, laughing, laughing, but there's nobody there to laugh, just pictures of people talking and falling down." Judit's assessment of modern television sitcoms was on the mark, as far as Betty was concerned. "I do not like tight walls around me, so I came outside. All right, all right. I will go inside my little cabin."

"And I will go home," Betty said. "Lord, I'm tired."

"Lock your doors well," Judit said. "There is evil abroad tonight."

"Don't I know it," Betty said.

"Wait," Judit said. "There is something I have that you need." She ducked inside and returned in a moment with a long object wrapped in a red satin cloth. "My husband gave this to me when we were married. It comes from centuries ago, and from a land we do not now remember. It is stronger than any gun. My husband used to tell me that it was to be used only to draw blood for the final sacrifice." She thrust the object into Betty's hands.

Betty, made uneasy by all this mystical nonsense, unwrapped the object and found a shining, curved blade with a handle embedded with gems.

"The evil black bird-woman didn't find it when she robbed me," Judit said. "Take it for your safety."

"I couldn't," Betty said. "It's a treasure."

"You will need it," Judit said. "The cards do not lie."

Having seen Judit safely inside, Betty drove home slowly, the knife on the seat beside her.

CHAPTER 17

HOME AT last, and not late at all. Betty was exhausted and could scarcely remember Judit's dire predictions. She parked the Buick in the driveway to nowhere, now that the garage was gone, and unlocked the back door. She stepped into the kitchen, but before she turned on the light, she stopped and listened.

Tina wasn't exactly like a puppy that would come bounding out to greet her every time she returned to the house, but the cat did habitually manage to uncurl herself and stroll lazily out to see if Betty's arrival meant a replenished food bowl. Tonight, she wasn't there, and that felt wrong to Betty. The house was almost too quiet, yet she had a sense of someone breathing, watching.

Betty backed out of the kitchen into the yard. She might rise to an occasion like Tommy's attempt at getting even at the school, but she didn't like feeling that if she walked into her own house, she'd be trapped by the four walls without a means to defend herself.

Betty looked around the yard. There was nothing there with which she could protect herself. There was a quarter moon and a little light from it, so she could make out the shapes of the flowers in her garden. The lawn mower was leaning against the side of the house, but that was not a promising weapon. Or was it? Just as a precaution, she quietly moved it in front of the back steps and leaned it over, so that the bar crossed the second step. If anyone was inside and came out after her, there was a chance the bar would trip the intruder.

Ted had said he would be at home. She probably should creep across the street and call a constable, if not Officer Bob himself. The tales of robberies in town came back to her, and she was more convinced than ever that someone was inside.

But wait. Rumor had been connecting the robberies with Brad. If that was the case, logically it was Brad who was inside her house. But she had nothing worth stealing. Even her computer was fairly low end. The jewelry she'd gotten from Sid was well hidden, and unlike Judit's gold chains, almost no one knew she owned jewelry.

But where was Tina? In spite of their often testy relationship, Tina was a constant of Betty's life, and she hated to think that any harm had come to her. Had she left her outdoors when she left for Tommy's house and the dance? Then she came to her senses. Missing cat or not, Betty was facing a suspected intruder in her home, and the more she thought about it, the more likely it seemed it must be someone who wished for more than a few stolen trinkets. It was someone who wanted to spill her blood, the way Linda Rockwell's blood had been spilled on her own bed.

There was too much getting even in this town.

She didn't want to be the last sacrifice, and she didn't want to be the one who made the last sacrifice. She had to visit Sid tomorrow. He'd be expecting her.

What were her choices, then? She could get back in her

car and drive away. She could cross the field to the Saks house, but Penny already had too much to deal with. She could go to Ted, but he might have retired and she didn't want to get him out of bed, when there wasn't much he could do to help.

She would have to handle this herself. Judit's long and lethal knife was still on the front seat of the Buick. Not really much defense against a gun, but still . . . Betty shrugged. You made do with what you had, and you did the job right.

By now, whoever was in her house would be wondering where she was. The lights of the car had indicated that she was home, yet she hadn't come into the house. Maybe someone would get curious and come out to look for her.

She retrieved the knife, and with it in her hand, she felt marginally more secure. Indeed, the hefty blade seemed to send a flash of power through her arm.

Finally she stepped boldly into the house and called out, "I'm here. What do you want?"

She made certain that she had her back to the open kitchen door so she could retreat quickly, avoiding the lawn mower on the steps. There was no answer to her call, but she heard someone moving in the living room. Then Tina sprinted into the kitchen faster than she'd ever moved in her life and twined herself affectionately around Betty's ankles. Also unheard of.

Well, she couldn't go on like this, playing hide-and-seek in her own house. She edged toward the doorway to the living room. The light switch for the overhead light was just inside to the right. She flipped the switch.

Afterward, she could swear that Raven hissed at her as

the light revealed her standing in the middle of the room, over the unmoving body of Brad Melville.

I must be calm, Betty told herself, as she noted that she saw no blood, no ghastly wounds. Brad just seemed to be out cold.

On the other hand, it was not easy to remain calm with a gun pointed at her, and Raven had the gun. Betty had the ancient knife, which was much larger than the gun, but that was its only advantage. Suddenly Betty was very, very tired.

"What is this? I'm not interested in any more dramatic moments tonight. If you want to shoot me, go ahead, but don't expect any magic moments to result. I'm just a re-tired lady who can type and file and fix the copy machine. I find you both evil and tiresome, Raven, and not at all interesting."

Sometimes insults work. The gun in Raven's hand wavered, and perhaps her confidence, too.

"This knife," Betty said, waving the formidable blade, "comes from the distant past when magic worked. It has a power that you can't imagine, and, dear girl, it is meant to be used for a sacrifice. Will that be you?" Betty knew that she would never be capable of using Judit's knife to harm anyone, unless it was a matter of saving her own life, but Raven didn't know that, so she took a step backward as Betty took a step forward.

"Your games are over, Raven. Playing with a young boy's mind, driving him to desperate acts, performing desperate acts yourself. I know that you killed Linda Rockwell."

"Phil was mine," Raven whispered.

"What nonsense," Betty said. "People aren't possessions of others. And you had no right to drive Tommy to do terrible deeds. I don't accept any excuses for that."

"It was Brad. He said he wanted revenge for what the town did to him."

"What he did to the town. It's still nonsense. Tell me something I can understand."

"We were powerful. . . ."

"What power? You're holding an old lady at gunpoint. If you shoot me, what have you achieved? And what did you do to him?" She pointed at the comatose Brad with her toe.

"I hit him, with a clock."

Sure enough, Betty's retirement clock was gone from the mantel and was lying on the floor near Brad. "Brad was playing games with my mind to make me lose my power. I had to silence his thoughts so I could get my magic back."

"I treasured that clock," Betty lied, feeling that it had served some purpose after all, but it made her angry. "Your so-called magic won't work on me, Raven. Please just put down the gun and go away. The police are looking for you two. I don't like the idea of being sacrificed to gain you a few hours of freedom."

Raven tossed her long black hair and took a step toward Betty, then another, the gun still in her outstretched hand.

"Enough," Betty said, and brought the knife down on Raven's arm.

She felt faint as she saw the gun drop to the floor and the blood begin to flow. She would have a hard time explaining that she felt almost elated as Raven crumpled to the floor. Judit had been right. The final sacrifice.

* * *

Sid was dozing when she reached the nursing home at midday on Sunday. It wasn't far from Hartford, so it was a good hour and a half drive from East Moulton. The home was an old stone Victorian-era house renovated to make spacious rooms for the residents, and there was only a hint of health-care facility in its white-tiled hallways and random pieces of medical equipment being moved from room to room. The big shady porch overlooking a green lawn was occupied by a cluster of residents in wheelchairs, some of whom recognized her and waved when she came up the cement walk from the street where she had parked her car.

She looked around Sid's room quickly. Orderly, no dust, no soiled linens. In spite of the pervasive smell of medications, and old, ill bodies, the place was living up to its reputation. The attendants always seemed warm and welcoming, and dreadfully efficient. The orchid she'd bought for him from Miho during the winter hadn't survived its travels from the house in Wethersfield to the nursing home. She'd get him another perhaps, but Sid wasn't much of a man for plants, although she did remember fondly his pride in the huge potted plant that had survived in the Edwards & Son office for decades, only sporadically watered, but regularly and heavily doused with cold coffee. She only hoped her new garden plants were as hardy.

Betty still felt shaky after her trying day yesterday, but the thought of spending an hour or two with Sid had given her strength to get on with the day, with life itself. The police had assured her that they had gathered enough evidence to show that Raven had been present in Linda's house and was the murderer.

"She's claiming it was Melville's doing," the trooper had told Betty after the major crime squad had done its business. "Some kind of nonsense about getting even with the town for something in the past. They figured Linda Rockwell wouldn't be too upset if Raven showed up at the house. It even seems that Melville used to spend a lot of time there. Raven said something about Linda putting the make on Brad and on some teacher that Raven thinks is her property, old boyfriend, I'd guess."

"But why did she come after me?" Betty asked.

The trooper shook his head. "Maybe she thought you knew more than you did. Maybe because you figured out what was up with Tommy, you'd figured out what was up with her. Maybe she just liked shooting at people."

"Sacrificing them," Betty said. "For some end about which she didn't have a very good understanding. She believed in magic, but as Judit pointed out, she knew nothing about it. She would have liked to be a witch, but my understanding of them is that they are wise women, not muddle-headed young people racked with bloody dreams of power."

"Well, she and Brad have certainly made a good start at upsetting the town. I hope she finds a lawyer who'll give her a good defense." Officer Bob had patted Betty on the shoulder. "And I hope the town gives you a medal. That was very brave of you to stop the kid from shooting like that. I hate to think what would have been the outcome if you hadn't understood and gotten there in time."

"Just doing my job," Betty said, bringing her mind back to the nursing-home room and the still figure on the bed. She reached out and touched Sid's pale hand, stroking it gently.

"Sid," she whispered, "It's Betty. I'm here doing my job as usual. Wait till you hear what's been happening to me."

His eyes fluttered open, and she could see the smile in them. She smiled back. The clock had been turned back as she'd wished. They were young again.

A CONVERSATION WITH
JOYCE CHRISTMAS

Q. *Joyce, you first came to our attention as the creator of socialite sleuth Lady Margaret Priam. But please tell us about Life Before Lady Margaret.*

A. When I graduated from Radcliffe, I didn't plan to be a writer. I wanted to be an editor and book designer. This inspired me to attend the Radcliffe Publishing Procedures course because I thought I would learn a trade and get a job; I didn't want to get an advanced degree and dwell in academia. I did get a job as an editor with a very small Boston publisher, saved my money, and trekked off to Europe to live in Vienna and Rome for a year.

I came back a different person and went to work as an editor at *The Writer* magazine, with the truly legendary Abe and Sylvia Burack, who really did teach me a trade. I got to work with the best writers around, I got to buy carloads of paper (literally tons of it, for the magazine and books), I learned a work ethic that I simply don't see today. And I learned to write letters, an area where the Buracks excelled. Abe died several years ago, but Sylvia carries on, and few are the authors who can resist her letters inviting them to write an article for *The Writer*.

One of my proudest moments was seeing an interview

with me in the magazine, later reprinted in the annual *Writer's Handbook*. An even prouder moment was presenting the Raven Award to Sylvia at the 1998 Edgar Awards banquet.

After *The Writer*, I went to live on a tiny Caribbean island for a few years. (I guess I don't stay put easily.) Finally, when I came back to Boston, I noticed that in that big college town, everybody seemed to be a college freshman—but I was not. So I moved to New York, where I freelanced as a copy editor, ghostwriter of a dozen nonfiction books, public relations writer, and advertising copywriter. I have always said, "If they pay me, I will write."

I took a job with a hotel technology consulting firm in New York, not because I know anything about technology, but I am able to write reports about technology that hotel general managers can understand. Now I edit a hotel technology newsletter, write articles for hotel trade magazines, and administer.

Q. *What was your first credit as a published writer?*
A. I believe it was "Three Little Kittens' Christmas," a one-act play for children in *Plays* magazine (another publication of The Writer, Inc.), a work that has been acclaimed as a forerunner to *Cats* and *The Lion King* without the money or the costumes. After ghostwriting nonfiction books, I wrote my first novel, *Hidden Assets*, with a friend, Jon Peterson. He won the coin toss, so it came out under the name Christmas Peterson. Two more unremarkable novels followed under my name, *Blood Child* and *Dark Tide*. Tattered copies of the latter continue to be much

beloved in my hometown of Niantic, Connecticut, since it was set there.

Q. *What was your inspiration for the Lady Margaret series?*
A. In an essay I wrote for *Deadly Women*, "The Aristocratic Sleuth," I discussed how I consciously chose to look back to the aristocratic amateur detectives of the Golden Age—Lord Peter Wimsey, Roderick Alleyn, Albert Campion, and so forth—and Lady Margaret was the result.

I happened to be working with just such a titled Englishwoman at a PR firm that promoted society/charity events, so she inspired me to use someone like her for my character. However, she is *not* Lady Margaret, even though her son has been heard to say after reading one of the books, "Mother, did you really do that?" So maybe I got something right about Lady Margaret.

Q. *You're a prolific novelist, but it was one of your short stories, "Takeout," that was nominated for a Macavity Award. How much time do you devote to short fiction?*
A. I don't spend as much time as I'd like. Short stories are a real challenge for me. I think good short story writers have a special gift, and I don't have it, so it's hard work. I write two or so a year, but I'm always thinking about possible tales to tell.

Q. *We know that you devise much of your own publicity and promotion: bookstore readings and autographings, in addition to appearances at libraries, Sisters in Crime events, and the annual Fifth Avenue gala called New York*

Is Book Country. How important are these promotional appearances?

A. I think they're very important. They give me a chance to meet readers and potential readers, as well as colleagues. If appearances can help independent mystery bookstores stay in business, they're worth it. Those mystery bookstores are a blessing for us who work in the field.

Q. *Also, each year you're an active participant, as panelist and moderator, at the major crime conferences [Bouchercon, Malice Domestic, the Mid-Atlantic Book Fair and Convention, and others]. Do you have a favorite conference or convention?*

A. I love them all, again because you meet fans and fellow writers. If I have a favorite, it's probably Mid-Atlantic because of its comfortable size and great organization (thanks to Deen Kogan, the founder of Mid-Atlantic). Malice Domestic was my first conference, so it has a special place in my heart. Bouchercon is tremendous and tiring. I also enjoy Cluefest in Dallas, and Landscapes of Mystery at Penn State, a new one that I hope continues, because I am devoted to Penn State football and its ice cream. There are several other reportedly great conferences I haven't had a chance to attend but will do so one day. I especially like conferences where I don't have to get on a plane but can take the train from New York.

The meetings of the International Association of Crime Writers that I've attended in Prague and Vienna have been wonderful. People in Europe tend to be suitably impressed by writers, and it has been very satisfying to get to know writers from other countries.

Q. *You've also served as a national board member of Mystery Writers of America. Was that a good experience? Did you derive any particular insight into the business of crime fiction? Any information/tips you can relay to other writers (or aspiring writers)?*

A. It was Parnell Hall who recruited me to run for the board, but I failed to tell him that I am not particularly good at meetings. Didn't miss one, though. What I learned was that writers expect an organization like MWA to solve all their problems with editors, publishers, agents, bad writing, reduced markets—you name it. Can't be done.

However, the mentor program sponsored by the New York Chapter of MWA assigns published authors to critique the work of new writers. I do it almost every year, including the mentor panel. It is one way I can help aspiring mystery writers. I support Sisters in Crime, too, and had the opportunity to moderate a huge panel at Douglass College [Rutgers] when the Sisters in Crime archives were donated to the Douglass Library, but given my aversion to meetings, I am reluctant to seek office, at least for now.

Tips? My only tip for writers is to read, read, read in the genre you want to write in, then read everything else. And practice, practice, practice writing. Revise, submit it, but don't wait around to hear the good or bad news. Start writing something else immediately. Writers' magazines like *The Writer* are helpful, and a lot of writers say that writers' groups have been valuable for feedback.

Q. *After numerous successful entries in the Lady Margaret Priam series, you devised another series and a new protagonist: retired office manager Betty Trenka, who* *debuted in* This Business Is Murder. *What was the origin of Betty?*

A. A lot of Betty's background comes from what I do in my day job: running an office. And I'm getting older, although not yet as old as Betty, so dealing with an accumulation of years interests me, always has. In several of the Lady Margaret books, I have older characters, and in my life I've been fortunate to have really close friends who are much older than I.

One example: My first boss was in his seventies and I was a wide-eyed new college graduate when I went to work for him. He finally retired at ninety-nine, but we remained friends until his death. Another dear friend was Hamlin Hunt, who was a well-known writer of short stories for the women's magazines of the 1950s. I think she was the person who gave me the push to become a fiction writer. My aunt Margaret was a feisty old dame masquerading as an elegant, refined Yankee matron. So I was eager to have an older character to write about. Betty's concerns and problems are more like real life than Margaret's, so the change of pace from one series to the other is a pleasure.

Q. *We've heard stories of your daylong fact-finding mission in the food halls of Harrods. Are those stories true? And when you sent Lady Margaret to the Caribbean in* A Perfect Day for Dying, *you surely must have done some on-site research. (How grueling!) What are your most memorable travel and/or research adventures on behalf of Lady Margaret and Betty?*

A. Research is the most fun part of writing. Margaret went to the Caribbean in *A Perfect Day for Dying* because I wanted to write about a place where I lived for a number of years. Of course, I did have to pay a return visit to refresh my memory. As it happens, however, life in the Caribbean is not all fun and sun. Behind the tourists with bikinis, golf bags, and wet suits is a third world country of poor farmers and fishermen and hardworking women who keep life going and raise their kids to be polite and study hard.

The islands are beautiful, but existence is a struggle, and the wonderful material goods seen on TV are all out of reach. By the way, in my six years there, I think I saw television only once, and knew only one family with a set. I spent a lot of time listening to cricket test matches on the radio, and occasionally joining the little boys in the pick-up cricket games on the beach. I throw like a girl, but they were quite impressed with my batting abilities. All those recess baseball games at Niantic Center Grammar School did me some good after all.

My favorite research adventure took me to Beverly Hills for *A Stunning Way to Die*. Then along the freeway to tour Forest Lawn Cemetery with a native Beverly Hills friend whose parents rest in the mausoleum, and to restaurants owned by my good friend, the late Mauro Vincenti, a genius restaurateur I met years ago in Rome near the Trevi Fountain.

Yes, I did walk the food halls of Harrods for several days to get it right for *Friend or Faux*, and I was taken to an old-fashioned steam circus which figures in the book. Before I wrote *Friend or Faux*, I had the opportunity to visit India, and pulled up that experience to write about the Maharajah and his wives and the country. I try to research everything so I don't make dreadful mistakes, and I use what I've seen and experienced. I'm thinking that Margaret will pay a visit to Rome one of these days, which will require me to pay a return visit.

Q. *Joyce, to conclude, let's offer you the opportunity to play both interviewer and interviewee. Go for it . . .*
A. "Is Christmas your real name?" That's usually Question One. And yes, Christmas is really my name. I was married to someone named Christmas and decided to keep it after the marriage was over. My birth name was Smith, and there are probably already too many mystery writers named Smith. Christmas puts me on the bookshelves next to Agatha Christie, but life in December is one long series of weak attempts at humor. No, I wasn't born on December 25; no, my first name isn't really Merry. You get the idea.

Here's another question: "What do you do in your off (nonworking, nonwriting) hours?" I read a lot of stuff—history, biography, and mysteries. I cook. I keep in touch by e-mail with friends all over the world. I sleep, I wander around New York. Since I have to travel a bit for my job, I get to visit a lot of interesting cities here and abroad. I buy a ton of vintage and modern costume jewelry and, of course, far, far too many books.